MESSAGE

in the BOX

Dawn Merriman

Dedication

This book is dedicated to my wonderful husband, Kevin, and my children. Thank you for always supporting me. Also dedicated to all my fans that asked for more Gabby.

-Dawn Merriman

Chapter 1

GABBY

The large black dog stands in the middle of the road, staring me down, daring me to pass. I'd been in the middle of a drum solo on my steering wheel. Blue Oyster Cult was telling me to Don't Fear the Reaper and my gloved hands pounded hard and fast to the beat. I was deep in the middle of a daydream about performing as a rock star drummer when the dog forced me to hit the brakes.

The animal stops staring and paces from one weedy side of the road to the other. I slow, hoping it will move out of the way. When my car stops, it stops and stares again. Its brown eyes peer through my windshield, begging.

The cross tattoo on my left forearm begins to tingle.

My bright and easy day vanishes.

I turn the radio down, my dreams of drum solos long gone, and pull my car to a stop in front of the dog. It begins pacing again, to the ATV parked at the end of a driveway then to the mailbox at the other side of the road. The pacing grows frantic.

Hoping no other cars will come at that moment, I pull over and put the Charger in park. Looking both ways down the deserted country road, I slowly open the door. The blast of spring air warms my air-conditioned skin, but goose bumps rise all over my body just the same. I love dogs, but I know better than to approach a large Labrador that is so agitated. The dog seems uninterested in hurting me. It whines and goes to the mailbox again.

The tingle in the delicate cross tattoo on my arm increases as I make my way around the front of my car.

Then I hear the moan and the faint cry for help.

The spring weeds reach tall around the

mailbox, but on close inspection, I see some of them have been crushed. I hurry to the spot. A slight ditch falls away from the roadside, choked with weeds. Something flesh-colored is barely visible through the weeds.

An arm.

I step down the slight ditch to the arm and the moaning man, preparing for a bloody scene. The man looks up at me with relief. I recognize him as a customer of Grandma Dot's. He has his hair cut there once a month, even though he has very few hairs left to worry about.

"Mr. Sickmiller, what happened?" I crouch beside him, careful not to slide down the hill. "Are you hurt?" Mr. Sickmiller has suffered from Multiple Sclerosis for years and it has racked his body into a painfully stiff, faded version of the man I remember from my childhood.

"Gabby, thank God it's you. I've been down here for a long time. I heard Herbie up there pacing and whining, trying to get someone to stop, but cars kept passing by."

I place my arm under his shoulders, thin and bony, and help him into a sitting position. "What happened?" I ask again.

"I was getting my mail when I thought I saw something." He points to a spot further down in the ditch. "I tried to investigate but lost my balance. I don't walk so good anymore, you know."

"I know," I say gently. "Are you hurt?" I search his body for injuries, but besides a large grass stain on his white t-shirt and a streak of dirt on his arm, he seems okay.

"Just my pride. Sucks being so old and sick that you can't pick yourself up off the ground."

He attempts to get his legs under him and up onto his feet. His oversized red Crocs slide out from under him and he falls again into the brush. With my help and two more attempts, he climbs on hand and knees up the ditch bank. Using the mailbox and my arm for support, he gets one shaky leg under him, then loses his balance. He lands in the road with a humph of pain.

"I don't think I can get up," he mutters apologetically. "Might have hurt myself that time." He lifts his head, and a thin trickle of blood drips from his nose.

I crouch next to him, Herbie crowds against his master. A faint sound of an approaching engine grows louder.

"There's a car coming. You can't lay here."

He puts a hand on the asphalt and pushes, but his body doesn't lift. "I can't," he says miserably.

The engine sound increases.

I jump into the middle of the road and flap my arms to get the car's attention. A police cruiser slows to a stop, a familiar patrol officer at the wheel. Officer Patterson has helped me on several occasions and doesn't look at me with horror like some of the other officers on the River Bend police force.

Patterson rolls down the window. "Everything alright, Gabby? I was just on my way home and saw the dog and your car and then you." I point to Mr. Sickmiller trying once again to stand. "Oh, man," Patterson exclaims, grasping the situation.

With Officer Patterson on one side and me on the other, we pull Mr. Sickmiller to his feet. He wobbles and shuffles in his red shoes, but manages the few steps to the ATV.

"I always drive down for the mail. The walk is too much for me," he explains after sinking into the ATV seat with a grunt.

Herbie dances around us, excited to finally have help for his master.

I rub the dog's head. "You saved him, Herbie, good boy."

Mr. Sickmiller's eyes are watery when he looks at the dog. "I don't know how long I would have been down there if he hadn't stopped you."

Patterson is checking out Sickmiller's pulse and giving him a cursory first aid look over. "Do you need me to call the paramedics, have someone come check you out? Looks like you bumped your nose."

Sickmiller brushes off the attention and wipes at the blood. His face has turned an alarming shade of red. "I'm fine, don't bother with me." He rubs a hand across his sparse hair. "Maybe I need a haircut today, though." The few hairs on his pink scalp stand on end. I happen to know Mr. Sickmiller is sweet on Grandma Dot. If anyone can make him feel better, it will be her.

Patterson looks at me and then at the old man. "If you both are sure, then."

Sickmiller attempts to snap his gnarled fingers. No sound is made, but the intention is obvious. "I almost forgot what I was looking for in the first place. Gabby, there's a box, a big box down the ditch."

I sense Patterson tense and realize that my tattoo is still tingling even though Sickmiller is safe now. I don't have a good feeling about the box and I'm glad to have backup here already just in case.

"We'll check it out," Patterson says.

We wait for a passing car that has slowed to a crawl and rubbernecks at our little scene. Patterson and I cross the road. From the vantage point of standing at the mailbox, the corner of a large box or trunk can be seen.

"It wasn't there yesterday," Sickmiller calls from his seat. "That's why it had me so interested. An old box like that, or a trunk, could have treasure in it." He laughs weekly at his small joke.

The way my arm is tingling, I don't think treasure is what we'll find.

Patterson goes down the ditch in long strides. I follow as gracefully as I can, managing to not fall on my rear.

The crushed weeds show the path the box took down the hill. It has landed bottom side up.

On closer look, it does appear to be an old trunk, maybe an antique.

Patterson looks at the box and up the weedy bank to the road. "Think it fell off a truck or was thrown down here?"

I think I wish I was anywhere other than in a weedy ditch with a mysterious box and my tattoo stinging.

"Let's turn this over and see what it is." I'm happy to let Patterson take the lead. The box is indeed a trunk, with a handle on each end. He pulls one of the handles and attempts to turn the box right side up. He grunts in exertion. "Heavier than it looks. Can you give me a hand?"

With slow steps, I approach the trunk, thankful I'm wearing my gloves, even if they are just thin ones. I hesitate before I touch the handle, my arm sizzling, and my mind knowing already that whatever is making the box so heavy is going to be bad.

Patterson holds the other side and is looking at me expectantly.

I close my eyes and wrap my fingers around the metal handle.

Chapter 2

GABBY

As soon as I touch the handle, the terror fills me.

I jump back with a startled shout.

Patterson eyes me closely, first with confusion, then with dawning understanding. He's fully aware of my ability to sense things when I touch certain items. He's even seen me work on a crime scene before, reliving the details of a double murder.

"Did you…?" he searches for the right word. I don't make him search long.

"Something bad is in this box."

"How bad?"

"Bad enough that I sensed it through my

gloves. Terror. I was full of terror."

"Do you want to touch it, like for real touch it?" Patterson can't meet my eyes. He looks at the ground with a mixture of excitement and fear.

"Not without Lucas here."

He thinks for a long moment, then says, "Are you sure? I mean, I can't call in the detectives to look at an old trunk upside down in a ditch."

"Then open it," I challenge him.

He squats and looks at the heavy lock on the latch. Even after its tumble down the hill, the trunk is intact, the lock secured. It's old, but none of the wood is cracked or giving way. "We'll need a locksmith," he stalls, fiddling with the lock.

I'm growing impatient, "Just call Lucas. He'll come."

"I don't call detectives directly. I can only call dispatch."

"I'll do it." I reach for my phone only to find my pocket empty. "Crap on a cracker, my phone is in the car." I push past Patterson and up the hill. The weeds are slippery and the ditch bank is steep. I hold onto weeds to steady myself. A few pull out in my hand, but I manage to climb up to the road.

"Did you find something?" Mr. Sickmiller calls from the ATV. I'd forgotten about him and his voice startles me. Since touching the handle all I can think about is that I want Lucas, need his steadying presence.

"There's definitely a trunk down there." I open my car door and fish my phone off the front seat. "Maybe you should go back inside," I say as I push the speed dial icon for Lucas.

"No way. This is the most excitement I've had in weeks," the old man replies, patting Herbie on the head.

Lucas answers with a "hey gorgeous." Just hearing his voice makes the shaking in my legs cease a little.

"I, um. I'm out on Grandma Dot's road," I stammer, not sure what to say.

Lucas's tone turns to business. "What's wrong?"

"I, we, Officer Patterson is here already. We found a box." I finger the necklace he gave me for Christmas nervously.

"Gabby, just take a breath and tell me what's wrong."

Bless this man and his patience.

"There's an old trunk in a ditch and when I touched it…." I feel a burn in the back of my throat. "Even with my gloves on, I felt terror when I touched the handle." I manage to whisper, conscious of Sickmiller close by and no doubt hanging on every word I'm saying.

I can picture Lucas rubbing his hand over his face as he sighs. "You think it's that bad?"

With a start, I realize Patterson is standing behind me and I jump. He mouths "Sorry."

I take a few steps away and whisper, "Please come. The box is locked and maybe it's nothing. I'll touch it and figure out what's inside, but only if you are here." I hate myself for the weakness. After months of being a couple, this need for another person is still new and uncomfortable to me.

"You don't need to touch it. I won't put you through that. Give me the address and we will be right there." I cringe at the "we," knowing that means my brother Dustin will be coming, too. We are getting along a lot better, but sometimes I wish that Detective Lucas wasn't a package deal with Detective Dustin McAllister. I glance at the mailbox for the exact address and give it to him.

"Don't do anything. If the box is part of a crime, we need to leave it be as much as possible."

"Understood. And bring some bolt cutters. There's a big lock on it."

After putting my phone in my pocket, I tell Patterson that we need to wait for Lucas and Dustin. "You said you were headed home, so you are off duty. You can go if you like."

"Heck no! I'm not missing this. I don't care if I'm on the clock or not. I want to see if you are right."

I scrunch my face in consternation.

"Not that I think you're wrong," he stammers. "I just don't want to miss anything."

"Everything okay, Gabby?" Mr. Sickmiller calls from his front-row seat in his driveway. I cross the road to the ATV.

"I'm not sure yet," I tell him. "There may be something wrong with the box down there," I hedge.

"Did you sense something?" His question catches me off guard. Ever since Grandma Dot convinced me to open a shop on the square in town using my ability to help others and earn a living, I am often surprised at the number of people that know what I can do. For years, I was seen as a freak in this town. I hid my gift from everyone, even my family. Hearing it talked about so casually and with such acceptance from this man warms my heart.

I want to take his hand in mine, but decide not to push my luck today. Instead, I put my hand on Herbie's head and look at Mr. Sickmiller with tenderness. "I did sense something. I'm sorry."

"Don't be sorry." He gives his knee a week slap. "Does that mean more cops are coming? Maybe that boyfriend of yours."

"Now Mr. Sickmiller, how do you know I have a boyfriend?" I ask in genuine surprise.

"Dot told me, of course. She talks about you and 'that handsome detective' a lot. Just last month she and your mom were hoping for wedding bells soon."

"You are as bad a gossip as they are. I'll have to mention to them to keep my private life private."

"Now don't be cross. We are all just happy for you. After everything you've been through this year, you deserve some happiness."

I'm saved from continuing the conversation by a River Bend police cruiser parking behind the one already here. "There's 'that handsome detective' now, I bet." Sickmiller laughs and slaps his knee again. "Didn't take him long to come when you called."

Without another word, I hurry away from the old man and towards the cruiser.

Dustin climbs out first. He gives me the briefest of nods and turns his attention to Patterson. "Did you see this box thing?"

My eyes are drawn to the dark-haired detective climbing out of the driver's seat. It's only been a few hours since I woke in his arms, but the sight of him makes the spring air feel warmer.

Crime scene, Gabby. Get yourself under control.

Lucas listens intently to the little information Patterson has. I can tell by his body language that he wants to touch me, comfort me in some small way. He manages to keep his professional cool in place.

"Did you bring the bolt cutters?" I ask.

Dustin returns to the car and takes the large

tool out of the back seat. "These should work."

"Let's take a look at this mysterious box," Lucas says. He allows Patterson to lead the way down the hill, then Dustin. He takes a few steps down the hill, then turns to offer his hand to help me down. I take it gratefully. The warmth that flows through my glove has nothing to do with my abilities.

"We each took a handle and tried to turn the thing over, when Gabby, you know," Patterson says.

Dustin finally turns his attention to me and gives me the briefest of concerned looks. "Step back," he tells me. "Let's turn this thing over." The men put on plastic gloves and take hold of the handles.

I'm only too happy to let them take over. Even with the three of them, they struggle to move the heavy weight.

A solemn silence falls over the four of us as the box lands upright. Either the box is full of books, stones, or lead. Or something much worse. The beauty of the trunk doesn't match the horror I know is inside. The top is trimmed in shiny metal that looks like it could be gold-plated.

Ornate plates decorate each corner. Even dirty, with weeds ground into it, the trunk is beautiful.

Lucas is immune to the trunk's beauty. "Cut it open," he tells Dustin.

Even the lock looks ornate and old. It's a shame to cut it open.

With a crunch of metal on metal, Dustin cuts the lock free. It lands in the grass and Lucas collects it and puts it in an evidence bag.

Slowly, Dustin lifts the lid. As soon as there is a gap between the lid and the rest of the box, a noxious odor assails us.

An odor we've all smelled before.

Decomposition.

Chapter 3

GABBY

At the horrid smell, Dustin drops the lid closed again.

I place my gloved hand over my nose and mouth in an attempt to block the fumes. Patterson coughs.

"Looks like you were right," Lucas says with a tinge of pride.

I didn't want to be right.

After the initial shock, Lucas and Dustin carefully open the box. Curled into an unnaturally tight ball is a man. His face is covered by one hand. A large gold ring with a red stone surrounded by smaller stones of various colors glints in the sunlight.

"Looks like robbery can be ruled out," Dustin says, pointing to the ostentatious ring.

Lucas peers closer into the box. The man wears dark jeans and a dark blue button-up shirt. It's hard to tell much more than that with the way he is jammed into the box.

"Is that blood in his hair?" Patterson asks.

Lucas walks around the box to get a better look. The man indeed has a bloody spot on the back of his head.

"Looks like a .22," Dustin says. "I don't see an exit wound, but we'll have to wait for the coroner to be sure." Dustin talks to dispatch through the radio on his shoulder and informs them of the situation. "Team's on the way."

"Shot in the back of the head. Maybe he didn't know what was coming." Patterson offers.

I watch all of this with as much detachment as I can muster. I already felt this man's terror when I touched the handle of the box that became his coffin. "He definitely knew what was coming," I mutter.

The three uniformed cops turn their eyes to me with concern. I cross my arms and rub at the goosebumps suddenly dotting my skin.

"Do you want to-?" Lucas points to the man.

"We can do this the right way," Dustin protests.

"And we will. But if she can give us some information now, we'll be that far ahead."

Dustin looks disgusted. Patterson looks curiously excited. Lucas looks hopeful. I don't like being under such close scrutiny. I narrow my eyes at Lucas, wishing he hadn't asked me outright. I would have volunteered, but don't like being pressed.

He sees the look I give him. So does Dustin.

"Never ask her for anything directly, Hartley," Dustin says with a barely concealed chuckle. "You'll learn."

I resent this more than Lucas asking me for help. Dustin acts like he knows me so well when the truth is despite being siblings, we've only been remotely close for the last few months.

"Don't pretend you know me," I snap, unsettled and defensive.

I take a step forward while pulling a glove off. "I would do it anyway, but not for either of you. I do it for this poor man shot and stuffed unceremoniously in a box."

I kneel near the box and close my eyes, centering myself to the seriousness of the situation. I open myself to the universe and say my usual prayer. "God, please let me see what needs to be seen."

No longer caring about the three men watching me, I raise a bare hand and place it gently on the ringed hand covering the dead man's face. Instantly, the terror fills me again.

Hard metal on the back of my head. I'm so sorry. I never meant it to go that far. A blonde I've let down. A girl and a boy that deserve better. The click and the end.

I hold my hand on his, hoping for more, hoping for a clue to his identity or to who held the gun to his head. The sensations play through my mind, flickering like an old movie. I focus on the woman with blonde hair, focus on any detail I might glean from the vision. I give up and remove my touch from him.

"He knew his killer. They had some sort of misunderstanding. He thought about a woman and kids. His wife and kids maybe? He definitely knew what was coming and was pleading. He kept saying he was sorry."

"Sorry for what?" Dustin asks.

I shake my head and get back to my feet. "I have no idea." I feel exhausted and defeated. I had brazenly used my gift to prove a point to my brother. I hadn't learned much to help with the case. Nothing useful. Not even the man's name.

Dustin looks at me skeptically, a hint of satisfaction twitching at the corners of his mouth. "Did you get a name?"

"No. I did not get a name," I snap defensively, pulling my black glove back on. "This isn't an exact science. I don't control what I see and what I don't."

"We know more than we did before," Lucas says. "Thank you." He's trying to be supportive, but I'm not in the mood for support. I'm angry and disappointed with myself. I look down at the man in the box, a sudden sadness filling me. Why was he executed and shoved in a trunk? How did this box get here?

"Do you think the trunk was thrown down into this ditch to hide it or do you think it fell off a truck accidentally or something?" Patterson asks the same question I was thinking.

We all look up the hill to the road. Mr.

Sickmiller has driven his ATV to this side of the road and is watching the excitement. When he sees us looking, he waves. I give him the smallest of waves back. "Maybe Mr. Sickmiller saw something," I say. "He is the one that spotted the box. He said it wasn't there yesterday."

"Patterson, you want to go get his statement? We'll need to talk to all the neighbors, might as well start now," Dustin says.

Patterson was off duty but eagerly marches up the hill to talk to our audience of one.

"What do we do now?" I ask.

"We wait for the coroner and the scene techs." Dustin emphasizes the 'we,' as in not me. "You should go to Grandma Dot's. I assume that's where you were headed in the first place." I bristle at Dustin knowing me well enough to guess where I was headed. Grandma's is only half a mile down the road, so it was an obvious guess.

"Maybe I was headed home from there," I challenge him, feeling grumpy and tired after my nearly failed vision.

"Your hair is a bit wild. I know Grandma would never let you leave the house like that."

I run a hand self-consciously through my dark curls. My fingers catch in a tangle. I hadn't brushed it yet today. I feel my cheeks pink at the sight my wild hair must be.

"Oh shut up, Dustin," I snarl, feeling foolish that he is right.

"Maybe Dustin's right," Lucas says. "The coroner is a strictly by the book woman. She won't take kindly to civilians on a crime scene. Especially one as odd as this."

I know he has a point, but hate being left out. I don't know what else I can contribute to the case, so I weakly agree. "You'll tell me what you find out?"

"I'll tell you what I can," Lucas hedges. This is one part of our relationship that I don't like. I am curious by nature and relentless when it comes to cases I might be able to help with. Lucas has a duty and sometimes that duty doesn't include telling me the facts of a case.

A fly buzzes my face and I swat it away. The body in the box has started attracting insects already. Maybe leaving isn't such a bad idea.

"I'll be at Grandma Dot's. We are going to take Mom shopping for her apartment. Not sure

I'm up for it now." I'm suddenly tired, bone tired. And thirsty. I hope Grandma has a Dr. Pepper in her fridge because I'm craving the sugar.

"I'll call you tonight, I promise," Lucas says, and gives my hand a quick squeeze.

I look again at the dead man, his face covered with a ringed hand. "That's an odd ring," I say vaguely.

"Surprised the killer didn't take it," Dustin says.

"Maybe the killer already has one." I don't know why the words leave my lips. I didn't see another ring in my vision, but I feel certain the ring means something. I take a closer look at the red stone surrounded by colored stones. "There's some sort of writing or a symbol on the side."

Lucas looks with me, covering his nose with his hand, he leans close to read it. "A horse head, I think." He pulls away from the stench of blood and decay. "We'll know more once we get the scene processed and we can look at it properly."

"She's here," Dustin says ominously, motioning to the black van that is parking at the top of the hill.

"That's my cue," I say. Truth be told, I have

no interest in dealing with Angelica Gomez, the county coroner. She has no use for me or my abilities and has no problem voicing her opinion out loud. My presence will only complicate the scene.

"Good luck," I call over my shoulder and climb up the steep ditch bank as quickly as possible. I pass Gomez on the roadside.

"What are you doing here?" she barks.

"I found the box with the body in it." I hope my simple statement will keep her quiet. She narrows her intelligent dark eyes and studies me.

"You sure find a lot of bodies." The statement sounds like a challenge.

"Just keeping you in business." Grandma Dot would not be pleased with my flippant response and lack of manners or respect.

Gomez humphs and turns away, her customary, long braid swinging through the air. Her short legs manage the steep bank with ease. I secretly wish she would slip just a little.

"Gabby." Mr. Sickmiller calls. He is talking with Patterson, still sitting in the ATV but back on his side of the road, away from the scene. "He says you found a body in that box I saw."

Sickmiller's eyes are wavery and red. "Is it true?"

"I'm afraid it is."

He pulls Herbie the dog's large head close to his chest. "Poor man. Do you know who it is?"

I shake my head, "Not yet."

"Can't you touch him and, you know?"

His belief in my abilities is nice but makes me feel worse for my lack of results. "I did that already." He reads the discouragement on my face.

"Can only do what you can do," he says pragmatically. He then looks to Patterson, "If you don't have any more questions, all this excitement has worn me out. I need to go lie down for a while."

"Of course. We're all done here," Patterson says.

"Come on, Herbie, let's go home." He starts the ATV and puts it in reverse. "Thank you for saving me," he says. "And for finding that poor soul in that box." With that, he turns around and drives up his long gravel drive.

"Like he said," Patterson says, "Thank you. Who knows what would have happened to him if you hadn't stopped. And that box could have laid there forever. Maybe that's what the killer wanted."

I brush off the praise. "You would have stopped for the dog just like I did."

Patterson shakes his head. "I doubt it. I've seen tons of dogs in the road, I would have made my way around him and continued on home."

Home sounds good. Not my house, but my home.

I say goodbye to Patterson and then my Charger grumbles to life. A few moments later, I'm pulling into the farmhouse with a beauty shop attached to the front.

I'm home.

Chapter 4

GABBY

There are two cars parked in the beauty shop parking area at Grandma Dot's. One I don't recognize, one belongs to Grandma's best friend, Mrs. Mott. I pull around and park by the back door porch. To my utmost pleasure, I find my mom sitting on the porch swing, enjoying the spring morning.

It's been a few months since she was released from prison and the transformation from the thin and pale shell of her former self to this bright, healthy woman is remarkable. She served almost fifteen years for a crime she didn't commit. Having her here in the flesh is still a shock, a sweet, precious shock that I'm happy to be getting used to.

I climb the four steps to join her on the porch. A black fuzzy blur jumps from her lap and dances at my feet. Jet, Grandma's tiny dog, lets me know he's happy to see me. I pick him up and join Mom on the swing, settling into the red floral cushions.

"You look tired," she says after kissing my cheek.

"You sound like an over-protective mom," I fake protest, secretly loving the attention.

"That's what I am," she says good-naturedly, bumping my shoulder.

"I am tired and thirsty." I look at the nearly empty glass of sweet tea she holds. "Is there more tea?"

"Always. Made some just this morning."

"I'll be right back."

I leave Jet on the swing, and with Mom's glass in hand, I enter the kitchen. The smells of childhood delight my nose and chase the last of the decomposition smell from my mind. The usual herbs and baking smells are mixed with the scent of cinnamon. A tray of walnut-covered cinnamon rolls sits on the counter, still warm and calling for me to eat them. I pull one off the tray and shove a large portion in my mouth. I nearly melt at the taste.

Visions, even ones that are as disappointingly vague as today's, take a lot out of me. I usually crave sugar and a nap after. Today the cinnamon roll is the perfect remedy.

I finish the roll, fill two glasses with tea, then take another roll outside to the porch.

"Oh good, you found them." Mom motions to the roll. "She made them for you. About an hour ago, she just came out of the shop and said you were going to need a little something special today. So she made the rolls."

Somehow, Grandma Dot always knows when I need something. She has a touch of my abilities, says they run in the family. As I take another gooey bite, I'm glad she had a sense this morning.

"So I saw a few cop cars go past a while ago and you are late getting here," Mom starts. "Nothing horrible going on down that way is there?"

I fill her in on the details of the morning, from seeing the dog to telling Mr. Sickmiller goodbye. I leave out the part about being flippant to the coroner. Mom doesn't need to know all my failings.

"You are so brave to do the things you do," she says with obvious pride. "It's so exciting."

"I wasn't brave or exciting today. I was basically useless. I couldn't even tell the guy's name. The only thing I saw was that he may or may not have a wife and some kids and that he was shot. We already knew he was shot and having a wife or kids isn't that distinctive."

"But you figured out he was in the box to begin with."

"Someone would have figured it out eventually. I don't even know how the box got there. I did nothing." I cross my arms and grip my biceps hard to keep the emotion at bay. Jet whines and sticks his nose in my face.

Mom quietly sips her tea, waiting for me to get myself under control. "I doubt the man would see it that way. Or his family that is probably missing him. You just have to trust that what you see is what you need to see."

"You sound like Grandma." I shift in the swing. "Never let me mope."

Mom laughs and it sounds like bells. "Gabby,

trust me, you mope plenty."

I suppose that's fair. Mom always seems happy, never bitter or angry or resentful. She had fifteen years of her life stolen but she just keeps smiling. I wish I had her easy sunny nature. I'm more thunderclouds and rainstorms.

I feel the need to change the subject. "Are you excited about moving into the apartment? I told you I would move there and you could have my house."

"I would never let you leave your house. The apartment above your shop will be good enough for me. I love living here, but I need to start my life. I swear it's only temporary until I can afford something better."

"A tiny one-bedroom above my shop isn't good enough for you?" I tease.

"It's perfect. I love the view of the town square from there. I just don't want to get in your way."

"I work downstairs. It will be fine. To be honest, I'll feel better having someone around. It can get lonely there when I don't have a client. I don't know why I let Grandma talk me into opening a shop where I do readings and touch things for people. I can't believe I've managed to pay my mortgage these last months. If I'm not careful, I will be losing my house and moving into the apartment with you."

"More moping?" She pats my knee. "Grandma says you're doing great."

"Grandma doesn't see my bank accounts. This is a small town, how many people need me to sense the history of an object or tell them where Great Grandma buried a can of cash in the back yard?"

"No one asked you to do that. Did they?"

"Just last week. I took the job. It was a tricky one for me. I ended up running my left hand all along the most likely places in the yard until I felt a tingle. Unfortunately, we dug up two long-buried cats in shoe boxes before we found the can of cash."

"That's amazing."

I hate to take the compliment. "The family was so grateful, they gave me a big tip out of the cash. It was a packed can and there was some jewelry inside as well."

The back door opens and Grandma Dot chimes in, "You telling her about Matilda

Haverston's buried can?"

"Uh-huh."

Grandma takes a seat on the porch and Mrs. Mott follows her out.

Grandma beams with pride. "Her granddaughter was in here yesterday and told me all about it. There was over twenty-five thousand dollars in that can, not to mention two rings and her grandpa's watch from working for the railroad."

"See, amazing," Mom says.

"You moping again, Gabby?" Mrs. Mott asks.

"Why does everyone keep saying that this morning?"

Grandma looks at my sticky fingers and changes the subject. "I see you found the rolls. I told Emily you'd need a little something this morning. After I saw all the cop cars go by, I knew I was right. Something going on down there?"

I tell the story of finding Mr. Sickmiller and the man in the box again. This time I add the detail about the ring. "It's quite distinctive. A horse head or something on the side, a red stone in the center surrounded by other stones in different colors. I've never seen anything like it."

"How old was the man?" Grandma suddenly turns serious.

"Not sure. I would guess about mid-thirties. We couldn't see his face and he was jammed in the box so we couldn't tell much. I didn't get a good reading when I touched him."

Grandma looks at Mrs. Mott for confirmation. "Short dark hair, just starting to gray at the temples? A large cowlick on the right side?"

"Maybe. Why?"

"Sounds like Jason Garafolo. He wears a ring like that. Hard to miss. He and his wife have come here for years. I remember the ring. God, poor Paula."

"He was thinking of her when he died. Curly blonde, right? And a little boy and girl."

Grandma shakes her head. "Paula has long dark hair and they don't have kids."

"Maybe it's not the same guy," Mom chimes in.

"He wears a ring like that," Mrs. Mott says, nodding and making her purple rinsed hair bounce. "I've seen the ugly thing, too."

"Maybe it's not him," Grandma concedes.

"You tell that handsome detective of yours what I said, though. I know Jason has a ring like that. Might help in some way."

"Speaking of Lucas, can you please stop talking about us to everyone in town? Even Mr. Sickmiller said you told him we were dating. You know we're supposed to be keeping a low profile because of his job."

"And you know that won't ever happen," Grandma says. "Nothing you do is low profile in River Bend."

Mom giggles, "If you think Grandma can keep her tongue from wagging in the beauty shop, you better think again."

"That will be the day," Mrs. Mott adds.

I drink on my sweet tea to keep from making some smart-mouth remark I will regret. Instead, I change the subject. "Are you coming shopping with us or are you working in the beauty shop?"

"I'm coming with you." Grandma motions to my hair. "Neither of us are going anywhere with you looking like that. Go inside and brush that mop."

Dustin was right.

I head to the beauty shop through the kitchen,

stopping to snag another cinnamon roll on the way. The woman looking back from the wall of mirrors in the shop is a fright. My hair is wind-tossed and the curls are standing up tall. I slept well last night, wrapped in Lucas's arms, but the vision and the stress of the morning have created dark smudges under my eyes. I'm almost embarrassed that I let Lucas see me like this.

I brush the curls into submission and pull the mane all back into a ponytail. I pinch my cheeks a few times to give them some color. When I feel I'll pass Grandma Dot's inspection, I rejoin them on the porch.

Grandma looks at my hair and nods her silent approval. "I was giving Emily one last chance to stay here at the farm with me."

"I think she wants to have a space to call her own." I look to Mom for confirmation.

"I haven't had any space to call my own for a very long time." A shadow crosses her face for a fleeting moment.

I lean against the porch rail and down the last of my tea. I'm uncomfortable with Mom's sadness even if it's for just a moment. She deserves all the smiles in the world after what she's been through.

"I'll drive."

"You expect us to ride in that grumbly car?" Grandma asks. "I'll drive."

"We will barely fit in the flatbed. Plus, where will we put all the new stuff we're going to buy?"

Mom puts an end to the discussion by pressing the garage door opener just inside the kitchen door. "I'll drive," she says proudly. The detached garage opens and a small white car sits inside. "I just got it yesterday." She's fairly beaming. "My very own car. I had to do something. I can't quite get the hang of driving stick shift in the flatbed."

"I know, right? How she keeps that thing on the road, I'll never know," Mrs. Mott says, standing. "I'll leave you all to it." She walks off the porch and into the sun to her car.

We pile into the new-to-my-mom car and I settle into the back seat. I check my phone for any information from Lucas. The screen is blank. "Can we drive past the Sickmiller place? I want to see if the team is still there."

"You want to see if your handsome detective is still there," Grandma teases.

"He has a name, you know." I strain to see

down the road. Over one hill and the scene of police cruisers and the coroner's van opens before us. "Maybe we should stop and check on Mr. Sickmiller." I'm itching to return to the scene.

"He's a grown man and he will be fine," Grandma says. "I know you want to be involved, but you've done all you can at this point."

The words are meant to be reassuring, but I take them as an insult. I have done all I can. Which is basically nothing. Even what I saw might not be true. If the man is Jason Garafolo and his wife is not blond and he has no kids, what did I see?

Mom drives slowly past the scene and I practically climb out the windows to see down the hill to where the box is. I want to tell Mom to stop the car. I want to try again to sense something.

As if she feels someone looking, Coroner Gomez turns and looks up the hill. She sees me with my face nearly pressed against the window, my neck craning. She gives a small shake of her head that I swear is disgust.

I sit back in my seat like a petulant child. I absently rub my tattoo with a gloved finger.

Maybe I've done all I can do today, but I know I'm not done with this case.

Chapter 5

DUSTIN

I watch Gabby climb the hill, hoping she climbs into her car before Gomez gets out of her van. The two women exchange a few words. I can tell by the set of Gabby's shoulders and the toss of Gomez's braid that the short exchange went about as rockily as I expected.

The coroner joins Lucas and me near the box, followed by several members of the forensic team. "Your sister has a bit of a mouth on her, doesn't she?"

Lucas presses his lips together to keep from smiling. "She's a little shook up after finding this box." I can't believe I'm once again covering for Gabby's big mouth.

"Right." Gomez snaps on gloves and gets to work.

She turns the man's head to get a better look at the wound. "Looks like a single shot. Most likely a .22 since there's no exit wound," Gomez begins. "Probably never knew what was coming."

I don't correct her with the information we got from Gabby. Either way, he ended up dead.

"Get this box up the hill and into the van." Gomez takes over the scene. "I'll work on it at the lab."

I lean back in my office chair and stare at the stain on the ceiling, deep in thought. Per Gomez's instructions, the body has been removed from the ditch, box and all, and taken to the Coroner's office for the autopsy. There was no identification on the body and no one at the scene recognized the man. Except for the gaudy ring, there was nothing identifiable about him. With him still in the box, the only things we could determine were middle age, medium build, brown hair, brown eyes. He's about as average as can be.

Lucas tosses a blue pen on his desk facing mine and breathes a sigh of disgust. "No missing persons report matching the man," he says. "Gabby said he was thinking of a woman and child before he died, seems likely they would be missing him by now."

"Unless Gabby was wrong," I say, carefully keeping my eyes on the stained ceiling, avoiding the icy glare I know Lucas is giving me.

"Has she ever been wrong before?"

"There's always a first time."

Lucas sighs and leans back in his chair as well. This is our favorite thinking pose, both of us staring at the stain, our minds racing. We solve a lot of cases this way.

"The only thing we have for sure besides the body is the ring." I bite my lip as I think.

"And the trunk he was in," Lucas adds. "It was far enough off the road, someone either carried it there or pushed it off a truck and it rolled down."

"I vote for it rolled there, the way it was upside down. Surprised the thing didn't break apart on impact. It was pretty old."

"They don't make things sturdy like that anymore," Lucas muses. "Can't be too many trunks like that around here."

"They sell them over at Draper Falls at the auction house fairly often. Alexis and I went last summer to the auction house and they had one. It was nowhere near as nice as this one, but they do have them sometimes."

"So anyone could own one." Lucas sits upright in frustration. "Wait, I think I've seen a trunk just like that one before. I remember the gold trim."

"You remember gold trim?" I ask incredulously.

"I went on a field trip with Olivia's class when she still went to school in River Bend. The history museum down on the square has a bedroom display with furniture and clothes, the whole bit. The trunk sat at the foot of the bed. I remember because one of the boys in our group snuck under the rope and was climbing on the trunk. I had to get him out of there before he got caught."

I sit upright and grin at my friend. "Did you get caught?"

"No. I told the kid if he hurried up and got down, I'd show him my badge. He said he wanted to pull off the gold so he could be rich."

"That kid's going to end up as a guest here someday." I stand up and head for the door. "Think I can trust you not to climb on any exhibits if we go to the museum now?"

"I wasn't climbing on it. The kid was," Lucas protests.

My phone chirps with Alexis' ringtone as we enter the hall. "Give me a sec," I tell Lucas, and duck back into our office.

"Hey," I say nervously. "I tried to call you earlier." I hate the ring of accusation in my voice. There's no rule that says she has to answer every time I call.

"Yeah, sorry about that. I was out."

She hadn't mentioned going out today, but she doesn't need my permission to do things. "Where did you go?" I want the words back as soon as they leave my lips.

"Just out, to the store, you know. Why does it matter?"

Why does *it matter? Because I don't believe her.*

"It doesn't. Look, we had a case come in this morning, so things are going to be nuts for a bit."

"Uh-huh." That's all she says. No questions,

no interest.

"A body. A dead man." I don't know why I'm trying to shock her, to draw some response.

"I figured as much." She sounds so distant, I barely recognize her voice. The gnawing feeling that's been in my belly for weeks grows.

"Anyway, I might be late tonight and wanted you to know." I pick up Lucas's blue pen and drop it again.

"We'll manage without you. We always do."

"Alexis?" I want to ask her if everything is okay. I want to ask her why she's been so distant, so different.

"Look, Dustin, Walker is fussing. I got to go."

"Love you." She's already hung up and I don't think she heard me. I rub my face and school it into a fake expression that belies my suspicions. When I feel the terror inside me isn't visible on the outside, I step back into the hall to join Lucas and visit the museum.

The River Bend Historical Museum is on the square downtown. It is located in the same bank of connected buildings as Gabby's shop. The courthouse sits at the center of the square, a mostly utilitarian building with a few sculpted flourishes. River Bend is not known for its glorious architecture and stunning landscape. Only where the wide bend of the river stretches into a lovely scenic view does River Bend really shine. The park there and covered wooden bridge are the jewels of the town. The square is a relic of a time long past. The McDonald's and the Walmart on the edge of town on Highway 7 are the future.

I prefer the square and its quaint little shops. Even Gabby's little business front, "Messages," seems to fit downtown.

We park the cruiser several spots from the Messages storefront and walk to the River Bend Historical Museum. The museum doesn't see a lot of traffic besides the occasional field trip from the surrounding schools and outings by older couples looking for something to do.

The retired-age woman at the front desk looks up excitedly as the overhead bell chimes on our entry. Her face clouds with confusion and a touch of concern when she sees our uniforms.

"Can I help you?" she asks as if she dreads

our answer.

Lucas turns on his charm. "I think you can help us." His eyes smoothly move over her gold-colored name tag. "Mable, are you in charge here?"

Mable's cheeks turn one shade pinker and she touches her hair. "Oh, my, no. I just watch the front desk."

"So you are in charge." Lucas leans towards her. "Everything goes through you."

Mable touches her hair again. "I wouldn't say everything." She lowers her voice to a whisper, "But Gene couldn't run this place without me."

"That's what I figured," Lucas continues, smooth as butter. I've seen him work this magic before. I'm never sure if his talent with the ladies makes me jealous or a bit sick. I suppose a little of both.

"Is there something in particular I can help you with?" She suddenly sits upright in her seat. "Oh, no this isn't about a crime is it?"

"Probably nothing. I mean, we just wanted to take a look at an old trunk you have on display here. At least you had it last time I visited."

"A trunk?" Mable looks confused. "We have

a trunk. It was part of the bedroom scene. It is in storage right now. We made room for that coin collection that came in last December. The new display has been a huge hit."

"But the trunk. Can we see it?"

"Of course. Let me think, it was put up in the attic, I think. Dear me, maybe you need to talk to Gene. He handles those kinds of things."

The sweet talk routine has run its course, so I ask as patiently as possible. "Can we talk to Gene, please?"

"Oh, he's not here right now. He ran down to that new place on the square. Messages. Have you heard of it?" Mable leans close and whispers. "The woman who runs it is psychic. She can even solve crimes."

"Yes we've heard of it," Lucas says sweetly before I can answer. "Is there a particular reason Gene went to Messages?"

Mable darts her eyes at the door and then into the deserted museum before whispering, "Things have moved around here."

Lucas and I just stare at her, waiting for her to go on. "Moved?" I prompt.

"At night. Things will be in one place when

we close and then in the morning, they are somewhere else." Her words drip with excitement. "Gene went to ask that nice lady at Messages, oh, what is her name?"

"Gabby McAllister," Lucas supplies.

"Right. He went to ask Ms. McAllister if she could find out what is haunting the museum." Mable looks so triumphant. "Just think, we could have our very own ghost here."

"If you have a ghost, Gabby will be able to tell you," Lucas says. "She's very good at her job."

Mable leans across the counter again, making ready to have a nice long gossip fest. "You don't think she's a little," she searches for the word and I watch Lucas's face for his reaction. "Odd. I mean someone who does what she does has to be a bit odd, doesn't she?"

Lucas fights to keep his reaction neutral. "She might be a little odd, but she's also amazing."

Mable suddenly leans away, "Oh, my goodness. I forgot she helps you all with cases sometimes. Do you know her well?" As if she can't help herself, Mable adds. "Does she really wear gloves all the time like they say?"

Lucas looks to me for help.

"I think we'll just walk down to Gabby's shop to find Gene and ask him about the trunk. If we miss him, can you please give him my card and have him call us as soon as possible."

Mable glances at the card and reads my name. I can tell by the redness of her cheeks that she finally made the connection between us and Gabby. "Oh my. I forgot she was your sister. I'm so sorry if I said anything impolite."

"You didn't say anything wrong. It's natural to be curious about her," I try my own brand of charm. "She doesn't bite, though."

"Of course not. I didn't mean that." Mable seems offended now. Guess my brand of charm doesn't work as well as Lucas's.

Chapter 6

GABBY

The handles of the plastic bags cut into my wrists as I unlock the back door of my shop. "You know it's only a tiny one-bedroom apartment," I tease my mom as I push open the door. "I'm not sure all this stuff will fit in there."

"Are you whining again?" Mom teases back. I manage to push open the door and press into the back entrance of the shop with all the bags. Mom and Grandma Dot follow close behind, their arms as laden as mine.

From my vantage point, I can see through the shop to the front door. A man has his face pressed against the glass door, his hands cupped around his eyes to block the glare. When he sees me his those eyes widen with excitement.

I nearly drop the bags in surprise.

Grandma pushes past me and sees the man, too. "Looks like you have a customer." She takes a few of the bags off my arms and starts up the steps to the apartment that will soon be my mother's. "Drop the rest of the bags and go drum up some business."

I set the bags downs and rub my wrists where the plastic handle left painful impressions. The man at the door waves when he sees me. His bulbous red nose and wire-rim glasses look familiar, but I can't immediately place him.

As soon as the door opens, he bustles in. "Ms. McAllister, so glad I caught you," he says breathlessly.

"Call me Gabby," I say automatically, stepping back so the man can properly enter the shop. "Take a seat and tell me what I can do for you." I motion to the dark red couch and two yellow chairs I use for meeting with clients. I'm conscious of Mom slowly making her way up the back steps, watching me work. I don't have to turn to see her to know that her mouth is curved into a look of pride. Since she has been home, I've caught her with that look on her face enough times I can sense it on the back of my neck.

The man nods towards the steps and the crinkle of plastic bags fades to the second floor.

He settles himself on the red couch and I take my usual seat in a chair. "I'm Gene Trimble, director down at the historical museum."

"Ahh, I thought you looked familiar, but I couldn't place it."

Gene looks confused.

"I've seen you walk by the shop or out on the sidewalk. I didn't know you're name, though. It's been a lot of years since I've been to the museum."

"But I thought you were…." He leaves the sentence open. The word *psychic* is hanging between us.

"Just because I can sense certain things, doesn't mean I know everything." It takes a force of self-control to keep from sighing in agitation. I've run into this before. He's not being rude, he's just ignorant.

"Of course, of course." Gene rubs at his red nose. "I'm sorry. I can't believe I'm down here asking you about all this. I never imagined something like this would happen to me or the museum."

"Mr. Trimble, Gene. Why don't you tell me what has you so upset."

"Right, right." He takes off his wire-rim glasses and rubs them on his checked shirt. "I'll just come out and say it. I think the museum is haunted."

I bite the inside of my cheek to keep from smiling. This is my first haunting inquiry. I personally don't know how I feel about hauntings. Sensing things is out there enough, but ghosts? I mentally shrug. Why not?

"What makes you think the museum is haunted?"

"Maybe haunted is too strong a word, but something is going on. I know the police will make fun of me and I didn't know who else to talk to."

"Gene, you haven't told me what the problem is yet."

"Oh, oh, I didn't. It's hard to explain, but it's a sense I get sometimes. Things seem to be moved overnight. I am very familiar with the exhibits, and several times in the last few weeks, I feel like they are different somehow. Nothing huge, just slightly rearranged. Like the other morning, the carnival glass display, I swear the pieces are in a different order than they were before. The small candy dish has always been to the left of the larger candy dish. Now it's on the right."

I have no response to moved candy dishes.

"I know it seems like nothing, but there's more. Sometimes when I walk into a room, I get the sensation that someone just left the room. Do you know what I mean? Or I feel like someone is watching me. I know what you're thinking, that I'm just an old man and I'm losing my marbles. But I swear something is going on. That's another thing. Marbles. We have quite a collection of marbles. Some of them are very valuable. We had three red Aggies and now we only have two. I know there were three."

He stops to catch his breath. His glasses have fogged with his agitation and he again wipes them on his checked shirt. "Gene, I don't think you're an old man losing your mind." I almost said marbles like he did, but changed the word at the last moment. "I, of all people, know the importance of trusting your gut. What would you like me to do to help you?"

He leans forward and says in a low voice, "Can you do a séance or a cleansing or something like that?"

This may be my first haunting inquiry, but not my first request to do a séance. Dustin would have a fit if I ever did one. 'no crystal balls and séances' he'd said when I opened the shop.

"I'm sorry, that's not how I work." I launch into my explanation of my abilities. "When I was fourteen, I was hit in the head," I start my spiel, touching the scar on my eyebrow. "I was in a coma for three days. I woke up with the ability to sense things." I pause here, letting the information sink in. "I'm not psychic the way you probably understand the word. I can't see the future or guess lottery numbers. I don't have a crystal ball and I can't talk to the dead. What I can do is sense the history of items or people when I touch them. I don't know how it works or why I can do it. Sometimes I can't sense anything. I don't control the gift, but I try to use it to help people."

I finish my practiced speech and look at Gene expectantly. He doesn't seem to understand.

"So you can help me?"

"I can try, but you need to know that I don't make any guarantees."

"I don't need a guarantee. I just need whatever is haunting my museum to stop."

I explain my fees and Gene agrees eagerly. "When can you come?"

"I have to finish something with my Mom and Grandma for a little bit, but I can come by later this afternoon and take a look around."

"Perfect, perfect. I'll see you in about an hour then?"

The bell over the door jangles and Gene visibly stiffens as Lucas and Dustin stroll in. With their uniforms puffed out by their safety vests, their tool belts jangling with a gun, cuffs, flashlight, and other essentials, their badges pinned to their chests, they seem imposing and overly large for the small space of my shop. Gene shoots me a worried glance.

"Gene Trimble?" Dustin asks.

Gene rubs at his red nose in apprehension. "Yes, yes, I'm Gene Trimble."

He looks so scared to be questioned by the police, I take pity on him. "Gene, this is my brother Detective Dustin McAllister and his partner, Detective Lucas Hartley. They won't hurt you. Mr. Trimble and I were just finishing a business meeting. What do you need his help with?"

"It's about the trunk," Lucas says. "You had an antique trunk on display. Mable says it's in storage. We'd like to verify that it's still in the museum."

Gene's eyes nearly bulge out of his head. "That is one of the things I wanted to show you, or I guess to tell you about." He takes his glasses off and on nervously. "The trunk disappeared two nights ago. It was in storage in the attic and now it's gone."

I meet Lucas's eyes and he nods slightly. I wonder how much they are going to tell Gene at this point in the investigation. "Would you be able to show us where you kept the trunk before it disappeared?" Lucas asks.

"Sure, sure, but what is this about? I didn't tell the police about the-," he darts his eyes at me, about to say haunting. I give a tiny shake of my head. "About the things moving."

"We rather not say at this time," Dustin uses his best cop voice. "Can you take us to the storage area now, please?"

Gene looks terrified to have the police questioning him. "Don't worry, I'll come, too," I assure him. I turn to Lucas, "Just give me a minute to tell Grandma and Mom."

"They're here?"

"Upstairs. Mom's moving into the apartment."

An unnamable expression crosses his face.

"You don't need to come, Gabby. We can handle this without you."

"Gene wants my help with another matter. I might as well look into it now."

"What other matter?" Dustin asks.

"That's between me and my client."

By the shift of his shoulders, I know Dustin wants to respond, but he doesn't argue the point. "Just hurry up."

I bound up the stairs to the apartment above and find Grandma Dot and Mom huddling at the door, obviously eavesdropping and making no effort to hide it.

"Haunted?" Mom whispers. "Is he for real?"

"Stop that," I whisper back. "There are strange things in this world that we can't explain." I hold up my gloved hands as proof.

"I suppose you've seen some crazy things. All in a day's work, right." Mom says. "You're so lucky to be part of this."

"Guess us old ladies will have to just wait here for you to return," Grandma teases.

"I'm not old," Mom protests.

I shake my head at the pair of them. Maybe it's a good thing Mom is moving out of Grandma's house. Too much time together can sour even the best relationships. I've noticed their "teasing" has increased over the last few weeks. Grandma wants to keep Mom close and safe. Mom wants freedom after all these years. It's a dance they went through years ago and here they are doing it again.

"Before you go," Grandma stops me. "Where'd the pillows go that I brought up here yesterday?"

I look past them into the apartment. "On the couch where you left them. I haven't even been up here since."

"They're not here."

"Gabby, you coming?" Dustin calls from the bottom of the stairs. "Hey Mom, Grandma," he says a little stilted. Mom and Dustin are still working on their relationship. For the years Mom was in prison, Dustin didn't visit or reach out to her. He was sure she was guilty. He looks guilty now, the same abashed look on his face he always has when he sees Mom.

Mom on the other hand beams at her golden boy. "I haven't seen you in your uniform before. My, don't you look handsome."

I get that he's her firstborn and I get that a mom's love is forever and uncontainable, but I still want to gag.

"Coming." I turn on my heel and hurry down the steps. Lucas is chatting up Gene, using his most charming voice. I could listen to his voice forever. Gene, on the other hand, doesn't seem soothed. He practically melts with relief when he sees me return.

"Right, right, ready to go back now?" Gene asks.

If he knew we were going to his museum to look for a crime scene, he wouldn't be so relieved.

Chapter 7

GABBY

The woman at the front desk seems startled to see us enter as a group. "Gene, is everything okay?" she asks, patting her hair nervously.

"These officers want to see where we kept the trunk from the bedroom display. Nothing serious." Gene assures her.

Mable itches to follow us. She stands, then sits again, curiosity obviously eating at her. I give her a small smile. Her life at the front desk of the practically deserted museum can't be too exciting and I know what it feels like to be left out.

She quickly looks away from me and pretends to be busy with some paperwork. I try not to take it personally. I'm used to odd reactions, but it stings a bit.

We follow Gene through two floors of the museum and to a door that must lead to the third-floor attic. I keep my hands pushed tight into my pockets, careful not to touch anything. I can feel the buzz of history in the building, sense the many stories the items have to tell. I haven't been here since a field trip years before the night I was injured and acquired my abilities. Generally, I avoid places like this.

Lucas looks over his shoulder at me, smiling encouragement. He mouths the words, "Doing okay?"

I return the smile gratefully, longing to hold his hand but keeping a respectful distance.

Gene opens the attic door, saying, "I was up here the other day and the trunk was there. The next morning, I came up to look for an old dress that I wanted to change out on the vintage clothing display and the trunk was gone. I thought maybe Mable had moved it. But that's ridiculous. She rarely leaves her desk."

We reach the top of the stairs and the attic opens before us. It's not actually an attic, it's just a third-floor space. Windows stretch down one side of the long room, dust dancing in the sunbeams falling on the wood floor. The majority of the museum's items are on display on the first two floors, but plenty of items fill the attic. A bed and dresser are shoved against one wall, a bright blue quilt is folded neatly on the bare, straw-filled mattress. "The trunk was here with the rest of the bedroom display that we took down a few months ago."

Dustin and Lucas scan the room. I know they are looking for bloodstains or any sign of a struggle. Dustin looks closely at the floor, searching for marks in the dust. The floor is clean. Gene takes good care of the items in his care, even those in storage.

I walk around the room, my mind open, listening for some sign of terror or anger or anything that would help the investigation.

Gene finally breaks the silence. "I hate to intrude, but are you going to tell me what this is all about? What do the police need with an old trunk? You said you were detectives. I have to tell you, I'm getting a bit concerned."

They ignore his concerns. "Is this the exact

spot the trunk was?" Dustin asks, standing next to the bed.

"Yes, yes. Right there."

Dustin turns on his flashlight and inspects the floor. "There are faint drag marks right here."

"Mr. Trimble," Lucas says politely. "Could you please wait for us downstairs?"

"Look, I've been cooperative, but these items are my responsibility. I want to know what this is all about." Gene's bulbous nose is turning an alarming shade of red.

"Gene, please wait for us downstairs," I chime in. "I swear I'll tell you all about this, but right now these detectives need some privacy."

Gene seems mollified by my assurances. "Okay, okay. But don't touch anything. I have a system here." He makes his way slowly down the creaking steps. Once we hear the door close, Lucas looks at me.

"Are you up for this?"

"Of course," I say with more confidence than I feel.

Dustin just sighs, resigned that I'm going to help in the only way I can.

I slowly pull off my gloves and shove them in

my pocket. I hold my hands up, palms out, searching. I close my eyes and silently say my prayer, "Lord, let me see what I need to see."

Starting with the place the trunk sat until the other night, I touch the floor. A small shimmer of emotion climbs into my hand, brief and bare, unable for me to name. I follow the faint tracks on the floor where the trunk was dragged across the floor. Following more by sight than by vision. To my surprise, the trunk was not taken towards the stairs, but in the opposite direction, towards a large wardrobe closet near the back wall.

My feet shuffle along, my eyes half-closed, my mind distracted by Dustin and Lucas watching me. At the wardrobe, I open the doors and peer inside. The interior is clean, both of dirt and psychic sensations.

"Nothing here," I say, dejected. "I'd swear the trunk was taken this way." Another false reading or at least only partial sensations in the same day nearly crushes me. I face the men. "I'm sorry, I thought I could be more help."

"Nothing at all?" Lucas sounds disappointed. I can't look him in the eye.

"I got a little sizzle of something from there

to here, but it disappears."

The detectives search every corner of the room, looking for blood, for disturbance. The area is clean.

"This must not be the murder scene," Dustin says. "At least we know the trunk was here and now is at the coroner's."

"Are you sure it's the same trunk?" I ask. "There're a lot of trunks in people's attics. This missing one might have nothing to do with the murder. Gene said things have been moved around the last few weeks."

"Is that why he came to see you?" Lucas stands close.

I glance down the stairs to the closed door, sure Gene is listening on the other side. "That's really between my client and me," I say for Gene's benefit but nod my head yes.

Dustin takes another look around. "I'm not seeing anything that looks like a crime scene here, how about you, Hartley?"

"Hard to tell with all the stuff up here, but it all looks neat and orderly." He kicks at the dust-free floor with the toe of his black boot. "Maybe Coroner Gomez has something new for us, a direction to go."

"Grandma Dot says that Jason Garafolo wears a ring like the one the body has on. He also fits the general description I gave her."

"You told Grandma?" Dustin asks in angry disbelief. "Let me guess, Mom knows all the gory details, too? Bad enough you're involved, why not bring the whole family along?"

My hackles raise in the way only Dustin can set them off. "If I hadn't mentioned it to her, you wouldn't have a lead at all," I point out.

"We would have figured it out eventually." His voice raises an octave in sarcasm. "I just don't know how we ever solved crimes until Gabby and Grandma Dot started helping us."

Lucas has learned over the years to stay out of the way when Dustin and I start going at it, but this comment pushes too far. "Hey, that's enough, you two. If Grandma thinks the man may be this Jason Garafolo, I am willing to take the leads however they come to us."

I take a steadying breath and focus on Lucas and not my brother. "His wife's name is Paula. She is not the woman I saw in my vision, the woman Jason was thinking of right at the end."

"Could the woman you saw be the killer?"

I've been thinking about the woman with the wild blond curly hair all morning, wondering who she is and why Jason was thinking of her and not his wife. "I didn't get that sense, more like a sadness when he thought of her. Of course, he had a gun to his head at the time, so things could be jumbled. Judging by my track record this morning, who knows if what I'm seeing is even true."

Lucas crosses the small space between us and takes both my hands in his. His strong fingers and reassuring grip work wonders on the rough edges of my pride. "You're doing great. If there isn't anything to see, then you can't see it, right? You found the trunk and Jason's body. Without you, he'd still be lying at the bottom of that ditch. And Mr. Sickmiller may still be stuck with him."

I meet his crisp blue eyes and let all the love for the man shine in mine. I want to kiss him, but this isn't the place and Dustin is nearby. In his grouchy mood, I'm sure he'd have something to say about it. As it is, he clears his throat rudely.

"Thank you," I say and squeeze his hands before letting go. "Did the canvas of the neighborhood bring up anything? A truck parked in front of Sickmiller's, by chance?"

"Basically nothing," Lucas says. "One person saw a bakery delivery truck real early this morning, but that isn't unusual. We'll follow up on it. I believe it was from the bakery on the end of this street."

"You didn't sense donuts earlier did you?" Dustin snarks. Even for Dustin before he and I started getting along, this is harsh.

"What is your problem?" I snap. "I thought donuts were a cop's area of expertise. Isn't that why Alexis is always trying to put you on a diet?"

From the pained expression that leaps onto his face, I realize I've gone too far. I'm pretty sure it has nothing to do with donuts and everything to do with his wife. I instantly want to apologize, but he doesn't give me a chance. He just storms down the steps, calling, "Hartley, to the coroner's. Gabby there's no way you are coming along. Gomez would eat you alive and then have us for dessert if we bring you to her lab. Stay here and play museum sleuth."

He pushes against the door at the bottom of the steps and a surprised Gene stumbles out of the way. His large nose is as red as his cheeks at getting caught eavesdropping.

"Sorry, sorry, Detective, he mutters."

Lucas looks at me with exasperation. "You know I have to spend the day with him and deal with his foul mood now. Did you have to go and say that about Alexis? I don't think everything is great on that front."

I'd gotten the same impression over the last few months. Ever since I found her passed out in her laundry room from pills and wine on Christmas Eve, things haven't been right between them. "I wish I hadn't said that, either. My tongue has a mind of its own and sometimes it doesn't think."

"Only sometimes?" Lucas teases, the crinkles at the corners of his eyes deepening.

"Okay, most of the time." I slap him playfully on the shoulder, the only act of affection I can do with Gene Trimble watching from the bottom of the stairs.

"We'll check out the lead about this Jason Garafolo. If it is him in the box, I am very curious to know why his wife hasn't reported him missing."

"You know I can't keep anything from Grandma. I'm not sorry I told her about the ring."

"I know. That tongue of yours again. Just please, please don't talk about the case with anyone other than Grandma Dot and your Mom. Even that is a super stretch of procedure."

"I'm a stretch of procedure and it has worked out pretty well for you." I try not to sound defensive.

"I know, and that's why you're here right now." He gives my hand a quick, meaning-loaded squeeze and heads down the stairs. "I better not keep him fuming in the car for long or he might drive away and leave me."

I follow a few steps behind. "I'll fill Gene in with the bare details. Then I think I'm in the mood for donuts."

Chapter 8

GABBY

Gene seems shaken when I reach the bottom of the steps. I put my gloves on slowly, stalling for time to figure out how to explain what we were doing up there.

"So, so are you going to explain? The detectives refused. Said to ask you."

"Let's just say that your missing trunk might have been used in a crime. We had to be certain that it was the same trunk we found this morning."

He nods towards my gloved hands. "Did you? Figure it out, I mean."

I nod sagely. "I know I told you I would investigate the strange happenings here today, but could we put it off to tomorrow? It's been a long day and I'd like to be fresh and at my top form for you." Mostly I want to investigate the murder of Jason Garafolo and not screw around with moved candy dishes.

Never mind that the candy dishes pay the bills.

"Of course, of course. You'll come by in the morning?"

"Maybe it's better if I come by tonight. You said the things were moving at night, so that would be the best time."

"I can give you a key and you can let yourself in. I'd rather not face whatever entity is messing with things."

I nod sagely. I still doubt the museum is haunted, but something has the man rattled.

"These are the dishes that were moved," he says as we walk towards the front entrance. "Over there is the marble collection with the missing Aggie." He suddenly makes a beeline for the coin collection. "Oh no," he exclaims. "Something's wrong with the coins. See that one there," he stabs a finger at the glass display case. "That one is a slightly different shade of gold than the others. I'd have to look at it closer, but I think it's a fake. You know better than anyone that the coins are all genuine." His voice raises in distress. "Maybe it's just out of order." He scans the display. "No that's the right order. What am I going to do? Why would a ghost exchange a real Spanish gold coin with a fake?"

"I'll look into it tonight," I attempt to reassure him.

He looks me straight in the eye through his thick lenses. "You do whatever you need. Sage the place, hold an exorcism, whatever it takes to get this place back the way it should be."

"Gene," I ask him seriously. "Why do you think it's haunted and not that you are being robbed in some way? I mean, if someone switched that gold coin for a reproduction, that doesn't sound like a ghost."

He glances toward the front entrance and Mable's listening ears. "I hear it. Footsteps where there shouldn't be any. I even once heard children laughing. I swear I'm not making it up. I've worked here for twenty years and nothing like this has happened before." He steps so close I can smell his aftershave. "I once thought I saw her," he glances towards Mable again. "A blonde ghost dressed all in white, a long flowing gown. I entered a room and she was leaving it. I thought it was a patron that stayed after closing, but when I hurried to the next room she was gone."

Goosebumps climb up my arms and a shiver runs down my back. He believes every word he's saying.

With the key to the museum tucked in my pocket, I return to my shop. "Honeys I'm home," I call up the steps to Grandma Dot and Mom. The door to the apartment opens and Mom smiles out at me. "Come see what we did."

I hesitate at the door, a little afraid of what the two of them might get into when left alone. Mom pulls me in by the hand. I love that she doesn't hesitate to touch me, to grab me by the hand. I don't get visions from those closest to me, and I have gloves on, but being touched so casually is something I'm still getting used to. Something I'm enjoying.

The room is filled with pictures. A dozen images of me at different ages stare at me from the walls. Pictures of Dustin fill other frames.

Pictures of Grandma Dot fill a couple of frames. There are even pictures of Grandpa Jerry from years and years ago.

I turn slowly, taking in the display. "Wow. It's like a room full of love."

"Exactly!" Grandma Dot exclaims. "This way Emily is never alone. She's surrounded by those who love her most."

"This had to be your idea," I say to Grandma. I recognize some of these from your house. I touch a picture of Lucas and me together. "You even have Lucas. How thoughtful."

"Well, he's part of my family, too. I may have gone a little overboard with pictures of Walker, but my grandson is so cute, how could I say no." Now that I look I realize that Dustin's nearly two-year-old son does dominate a lot of the room. I have to agree, though, he's darling. I search every frame, but besides a small wedding picture, Alexis is absent from the walls.

Grandma reads my mind. "I don't have any of her, besides the wedding shot. Strange."

I take a moment to let the display sink in. It's a little overwhelming to see all the eyes watching me, even when some are of me. "It's wonderful,"

I breathe.

Mom smacks her hands together. "I knew you'd like it. We should do the same thing at your house. Your blank walls are a little discouraging."

"I have that one picture of the beach scene," I protest.

"One cheap painting is not the same thing."

"You just worry about your apartment and let me worry about my house. I like it empty. Makes things easier for me." I hold up my hands. "Nothing to worry about touching."

"Speaking of touching, how did it go down at the museum?" Grandma asks.

"Not too well. I was warned by Dustin to not talk about it. There isn't much to talk about." I chew on the corner of my lip, thinking about the bakery truck seen this morning near Sickmiller's. "Did either of you see a bakery delivery truck by the house this morning?"

The women look at each other then shake their heads no. "Why?"

"Someone saw a truck from the bakery here on the corner out early this morning. I didn't think that was a normal route for the truck. You two ready for a break?"

"You want donuts don't you?" Grandma says, picking up her purse.

"You know me too well."

The luscious smell of the bakery fills my senses as we enter the lovely shop. I've become a bit of a regular here. In the mornings when they are doing most of the baking, the wonderful smells waft down to my shop. Like a siren song, I follow the scent and order something. The cream-filled long johns have become a favorite treat. Making a mental note to take an extra run this week, we belly up to the wooden bar and place our orders.

"Is Mitzie around?" I ask the young girl that serves us.

"She's in the back. I'll tell her you're here."

I carefully remove my right glove and pick up the heavenly confection placed before me. I'm working on a large mouthful when Mitzie, the owner, appears.

"Gabby, glad to see you again," she says with genuine pleasantness. "This must be your mother. We've heard so much about you. How wonderful that justice was finally served for you." Mom smiles in response, her mouth full of donut.

"Mitzie, how's business?" Grandma Dot asks. The two women, of course, know each other. It's hard to find someone Grandma doesn't know in River Bend.

"Been good." Mitzie focuses on me. "Lila said you needed me?"

I swallow the last of the donut and clear my throat. "I wanted to ask about any deliveries you made this morning."

Mitzie's face scrunches. "We didn't make any deliveries this morning. The truck hasn't even moved in a few days."

"You weren't out by the beauty shop really early this morning?"

Mitzie shakes her head. "Not us. What's this about?"

"Does anyone ever borrow the truck? Could someone take the keys?"

"I suppose so. They're hanging on a hook in the office. Gabby, you're starting to scare me. What's up?"

Grandma Dot swoops in to save me. "I thought I saw the truck this morning and I wondered if you were doing home deliveries."

Mitzie doesn't seem to buy the story completely but lets it slide. "Home deliveries of donuts. I suppose they deliver everything else these days. Maybe it's something I should look into." Her eyes take on a faraway look as if she's contemplating the idea.

"Always the entrepreneur," Grandma Dot says. "That's what I love about you." Grandma has worked her magic and Mitzie has forgotten all about my truck questions.

Discouraged, I finish my donut. The last bites are nowhere as wonderful as the first bites were. So far I've made no progress on the case.

I can only hope Lucas and Dustin are having better luck.

I lick a stray bit of frosting off my thumb as we walk back towards my shop. "I love that place," Mom is saying. "Do you think Mitzie needs any help? I used to love baking. A job like that would be great."

"If she starts doing deliveries, she might," Grandma says.

I'm searching my fingers for any last sticky

residue before sliding my glove back on, so I don't immediately see the perfectly styled blond hair and the heavily made-up face waiting for me at the shop door with a cameraman.

When I see her, I freeze, wanting to turn and run.

"When did Lacey Aniston come back to town?" I say stiffly. "I thought she was in Indianapolis working at some big news station."

"You didn't hear?" Grandma gushes. "She got fired. Her dad had to pull some strings to get her old job back at the local station."

The three of us stand stock still on the sidewalk. So far Lacey hasn't spotted us.

"Just turn slowly and we'll go around back." I turn, but not fast enough.

"Gabby McAllister, I see you, so don't go trying to hide from me." Lacey's voice shrieks down the street. Passers-by turn to look. My shoulders slump.

"Make sure to talk to her with your sign behind you. Free publicity," Grandma says.

"How exciting. She wants to put you on the news," Mom says.

"Yeah, really exciting. She'll twist my words

and make me look stupid."

"Just play the game, Gabriella. You've done this before."

I plaster on a fake smile and turn to face the local reporter and my least favorite person, Lacey Aniston.

Chapter 9

GABBY

"Lacey, it's you." That's as much politeness I can manage.

Grandma tugs on my hand, pulls me in front of the shiny gold letters on my shop front window. "Messages" glitters behind me. Lacey and her camera lurk in front of me. I feel trapped.

"Dorthea, Emily." Lacey greets my family. Everyone in town calls Grandma Dot. Only Lacey would dare to call her by her full name.

Grandma gives her a smile that doesn't reach her eyes. Mom is grinning, enjoying the show.

"Heard you got canned." I toss the first verbal blow.

Lacey pales beneath her heavy makeup. "I decided for myself that Indianapolis was not for me. River Bend is my home."

"Lucky Daddy got your job back."

Mom pokes me in the ribs and gives me a warning look to play nice. That didn't work when I was a kid, it won't work now.

"I don't need to go to Indianapolis when you are here stirring up trouble for me to report on. You make the best news, you know."

"I don't stir trouble. I only help." I lift my chin in defiance.

"And I only report the news." She tosses her straightened blond hair.

Lacey signals her cameraman and he zooms closer on my face. "This is Lacey Aniston with River Bend news and I'm here with local psychic and amateur sleuth Gabriella McAllister." The way she says my name makes my stomach twist. "Gabriella, can you confirm that you found the body of an unknown male this morning?"

I stare straight into the camera, refusing to answer. Dustin will have a real and true fit if I comment on the news about the case. "No comment."

Lacey slides on. "We've already interviewed the property owner where the body was found.

He told us that you found an old trunk in a ditch and it had a body in it. Do you deny this fact?"

"I stopped to help a friend and a trunk was found. That is true." I hedge.

Lacey gives the cameraman the "cut" signal. He turns the camera away from me and Lacey leans in close.

"Listen here, Gabby. I need this story and I will get it from you one way or another. You can either tell me what I want to know now or I can make you look even worse than I normally do. So start talking. Do we understand each other?" She's so close, I can smell the lingering remnants of wine.

"I understand that you're not above making up news for a story. Must not be going too well for you if you drank your lunch."

Lacey pales and lifts a carefully manicured hand to her mouth. "You're a real piece of work, Gabby. A man is dead and the public deserves to know what you know."

I'm suddenly conscious of Grandma Dot and Mom watching my little showdown. Grandma wanted me to use this opportunity for some free publicity. Up close, I can see the tint of red in

Lacey's eyes. I'm shocked when a twinge of sympathy tingles inside my chest.

"I'll talk," I say quietly.

Lacey flashes a smile so quickly, I feel fooled and angry. "Wonderful. Let's start from the top."

Grandma pulls me to a better position in front of my sign. I run a hand over my unruly dark curls.

"I'm here with," Lacey starts.

I interrupt. "If you call me Gabriella one more time, I will go inside and not talk to you."

Her eyes narrow, but Lacey nods.

"I'm here with local psychic, Gabby McAllister. Word around town is you had some excitement this morning, Gabby."

I feel sick playing this game, but with Grandma and Mom watching and hoping I don't blow it, I open my mouth and will nice words to come out. Dustin and Lucas will not be pleased, but maybe I can make them understand. "It was an interesting morning," I say, "And a sad one. I stopped to help a friend in need and found a trunk on the side of the road. Unfortunately, the body of a dead man was in the trunk."

"That is unfortunate. Tell us, Gabby, how did

you know there was a body in the box?"

I flick my eyes at Grandma for support. I really don't want to say this. She nods to the sign behind me. For her, I continue. "I can sense things when I touch certain items, especially things that have a strong emotional component. When I touched the box, I felt that something terrible had happened."

"You sensed the murder?" Lacey asks breathlessly.

"In a way," I hedge. "I sensed something was wrong."

"So you know who the killer is? Why aren't you telling the police?"

Lacey had been playing nice, so the question shocks me. "I don't know who the killer is," I say stiffly. "And the police were there already."

"The police were already there and you didn't sense who the killer is? Did you get any useful information from your vision?" She makes vision sound like a nasty word.

"Not yet." I feel my face burn and hope the camera isn't picking up on my heightened color.

"Will you continue to be part of the investigation, or will you stay out of the way and let the police do their job this time?" Lacey's smile shows most of her straight teeth and she looks uncannily like a wolf about to eat my face off.

I struggle for control, struggle not to slap that grin away. If Grandma and Mom weren't watching, I might tackle her right here on the sidewalk, camera or no camera. That would give her a story to remember.

"I will assist in any way the police need me," I say simply. "All I am interested in is justice for the poor man and closure for his family." I school my face into an appropriately contrite expression. A far cry from the leer Lacey was wearing. "Now if you will excuse me, I have other clients to attend to." I nod to my sign. "I help others here at my shop. Help them solve their family mysteries."

Lacey isn't interested in hearing me talk about my shop. She turns to the camera and signs off. "This is Lacey Aniston with River Bend News."

The cameraman lowers the lens. My job done, I open the door to my shop and escape.

Mom hoots with excitement once we are inside. "Gabby, you nailed it! Way to go."

I warm at the praise. "It was all I could do to keep my cool, I assure you. That Lacey gets on my last nerve."

"You did great, Gabriella. Way to plug the shop there at the end."

"Just doing what you recommended." I wander to the yellow chair and drop heavily into it. "The problem is, she wasn't wrong. I am no help in this investigation. I hate not being able to do more." I let out a small sound of laughter. "Dustin is going to kill me."

"Why?" Mom asks, honestly confused. "Won't he be proud of you for being on the news?"'

I love her innocence, but she missed the past cases where me being on the news was not a good thing. "He's already mad that I told you two about finding the body. He told me to keep my lip zipped."

"Since when do you do what Dustin tells you?" Grandma asks.

"I'm trying to be more understanding. He has a job to do. I have a job to do. Sometimes those two things work well together. Sometimes they don't. But we've been getting along and I'd like to keep it that way."

Mom seems genuinely confused by the dynamic between us. "You don't give him enough credit," she says. "Besides, he's not upset with you, he's bothered by something else lately."

"I've noticed. He's grouchy as a hungry bear. And I've been an angel."

Grandma laughs out loud. "You are a lot of things, but you are no angel."

The afternoon sun drenches me through the shop window, the warmth making me tired. I let out a long and loud yawn.

"I wondered when you'd crash," Grandma says. "Two visions in one day, finding a body, dealing with Lacey. Why don't you go home and get some rest."

The chair I'm sunk into invites me to stay right where I am. "I have to investigate the museum tonight," I say sleepily. "Maybe a nap would be a good idea. I promised to be at my best tonight for Gene." I let my eyes drift closed.

Grandma has other plans. "Come on, get up and go home." She pushes against my legs. "You don't have any clients this afternoon do you?"

"No," I say over a yawn.

"Then get out. We have a few things to finish upstairs and then we'll let ourselves out."

Upstairs. I'd forgotten they were moving Mom's stuff in today. "Will you be sleeping here tonight?"

Mom glances at Grandma for confirmation. "I was thinking about it. If you have to work tonight, though, maybe tomorrow would be better."

"It's not a big deal. I probably won't even come here. I have the key to the museum, I'll just let myself in over there."

"You're going alone?" Mom seems concerned.

"I was planning on it. Want to come?"

Mom nearly bounces with excitement. "Come on a ghost hunt? I wouldn't miss it."

"I'll be back around 11:00. Does that work?"

She claps her hands together, "What should I wear?"

Chapter 10

LUCAS

Dustin pointedly checks the time on his phone when I climb into the cruiser after saying goodbye to Gabby. "Don't start with me, too," I say. "I was only a minute. I know you're looking forward to meeting with Gomez as much as I am. Which is not at all."

"Gomez is okay. She just likes things her way." Dustin puts the cruiser into drive and leaves the downtown square. In too short a time, we are walking into the coroner's office. The thick scent of antiseptic and sadness assails my nose. Rocko, the young man working at the front desk, greets us with unusually high energy. "Detectives, glad you're here. She's been in a snit all day." He says conspiratorially. I've only met the man a handful of times and we are not the 'gossip about our bosses' type of friends. His unprofessionalism irks me.

"I'm sure she has a reason." I think I know the reason, Gabby's presence at the crime scene.

I mentally brace myself for the upcoming meeting. Visits to the coroner's are never easy. Something about a body, clean and laid out on display feels disrespectful and wrong. The work is vital, but I wish I didn't have to be present. It's my duty to the dead to be here. A duty I take seriously.

Rocko escorts Dustin and me down a series of hallways, then stops at a gray, metal door. He puts his hand on the knob and it makes a small sound.

"That better be you with the detectives, Rocko." Gomez calls from inside the room.

"Don't say I didn't warn you," he whispers. Without another word, he swings the heavy door open then walks away.

Gomez turns from a computer screen on a counter, her long braid swinging with the quick movement of her head. "Glad you could finally join me," she says. I force my lips into what I hope is a pleasant expression.

"We were following up on a lead." I hate that I feel the need to explain myself to this woman.

"You mean, following up on your girlfriend." She turns sharply back to the screen. "What you do on your time, is your business, Detective Hartley. I do not want that woman touching my bodies." She faces me with all five feet of her stature held tight.

A sizzling response coils in my belly. Dustin saves me from making the mistake of saying the words.

"Why don't we just discuss the case and not this morning's events," he says with surprising tact. "What have you got for us?"

Gomez falls into professional mode. "First off, he had a wallet and ID in his pocket. Whoever killed him must not have wanted to hide his identity." She hands Dustin a plastic bag with the wallet in it. "Jason Garafolo, age 34."

I refuse to let my lips smile at the fact that Gabby and Grandma Dot were right about the man's identity. Gomez darts sharp eyes at me. "Something funny, about that, Detective."

"Nothing funny about any of this." I feel like a kid caught with a cookie.

"Single gunshot wound three inches behind the left ear. No exit wound. The bullet was found still inside the skull. Looks to be a small caliber. Most likely a .22. I've already sent it off to ballistics."

We already knew all of this. I'm not sure what I hoped Gomez would find. Maybe a handwritten "I did it" on the man's chest. Something concrete. The beginning of an investigation always leaves me feeling lost at sea and a little sick. So many options and no real direction to follow.

"What about the ring? Did he have any other jewelry?" Dustin asks.

Gomez hands him two more plastic evidence bags. "The unusual ring with the colored stones around the central red stone and a plain silver wedding band." Dustin glances at the rings then hands all three evidence bags to me to hold.

Gomez leads us to the body, covered by a sheet. "I haven't started the full autopsy, mind you, but based on temperature and lividity, I'd say he was killed last night between midnight and four am. His stomach contents showed he most likely ate dinner around seven o'clock. Nothing interesting there. At some point, not long before he died, he must have wanted a snack."

"A snack?" I ask.

"He had barely digested pastry in his stomach."

"Like from a bakery?"

"That's where they make pastries."

"A bakery delivery truck was seen near where the body was found."

Gomez thinks this over. "Could be coincidence, if I believed in coincidence." She moves to the feet of the man on the table. "Last thing I have to show you at this point." She pulls back the sheet, exposing the man's naked feet and lower legs. He has a tattoo on his right calf."

In unison, Dustin and I lean closer. I don't recognize the red and blue logo on Jason Garafolo's leg. "What is it?"

"It was not well done, so it's faded and bled, but I recognize the horse's head and the colors. It's a school logo. From Hartman College."

"In Anderson?"

"That's the one. I had an intern from there once. She was brilliant, if a bit too interested in men for my taste. She had a keychain with that logo on it."

I take out my cell phone and snap a picture of the Hartman College tattoo. "Must have loved his school. His ring has the same horse head on it."

"I loved Purdue, but you won't find a Boilermaker inked anywhere on my body," Gomez says. "Tattoos are for the simple-minded."

I think of Gabby's cross tattoo on her inner forearm and what it represents. There's nothing simple about any of that.

"Hey, I've got a tattoo." Dustin protests. "Walker's footprint and birthdate on my shoulder."

"That's different. You're not likely to change your mind about loving your son. I wonder how Mr. Garafolo felt about his school this many years after graduating. Probably regretted the drunken binge that led to the inking in the first place."

I've had enough of Gomez and her negative attitude. "Maybe it meant something to him." I defend the dead man lying between us. "Who are we to judge?"

Gomez's eyes narrow a fraction. "I suppose you're right, Detective." Her tone leaves no doubt she doesn't agree with me.

"Let's go talk to Paula Garafolo," I say to Dustin, anxious to escape the noxious smells and noxious attitude.

With the evidence bags clutched tight in my fist, I leave the lab. I'd rather deliver the news about losing her husband than listen to Angelica Gomez spout off her opinions.

The Garafolo's reside close to the neighborhood where Gabby lives. Smallish houses are neatly kept, full of couples starting out or couples in retirement. We park on the street and scan the neighborhood before getting out of the car. One white shutter hangs askew, bright and obvious against the red brick. Yellow tulips are scattered haphazardly in the built-in flower box below the windows. The house has the air of just beginning to slide into disrepair. I know next to nothing about Jason Garafolo, but I get the impression he's not much of a handyman.

A curtain moves behind the yellow tulips. Paula knows the police are here. A rush of sympathy for the woman fills my bones. I can't imagine what it must feel like to know your husband should be home and the police arrive.

Without speaking, Dustin and I walk up the cracked sidewalk. The door opens before I can push the bell.

A disheveled brunette fills the small crack created by the open door. "He's in jail, isn't he?" she asks without saying hello.

"Paula Garafolo?" She nods. "Can we please come in?"

She lets go of the door and backs into the room, shadowed despite the afternoon sun. "If he's in jail, you can just keep him this time. I've had enough." She paces the small room, pulling on the hem of her t-shirt.

"Mrs. Garafolo, please sit down."

She doesn't stop pacing, pulls harder on her hem. "I don't want to. I don't want to hear it." Panic touches her words. "Just tell me he's in jail. That's all I want to hear."

I step in front of her, blocking the path of her pacing. "Paula, I'm sorry." She stops in her tracks, pulls the hem of her shirt to her face. "Jason is dead."

"You lie!" she screams suddenly. "He's in Vegas or Atlantic City. He went to the Casino up in Michigan. He's not dead."

She backs away from me, stepping blindly into the floral couch. She falls backward onto the cushions.

"He was found this morning. His ID was in his pocket. We are sure." Dustin says.

"I thought," she sniffles and wipes her eyes with her shirt. "He's disappeared before. I just thought he was on a bender again. How did he die? Car accident?"

I take a deep breath before saying quietly. "He was murdered."

She pulls a decorative pillow embroidered with a blue flower to her face and wails into it. "Murdered? Murdered?" She holds the pillow to her chest. "I knew they'd catch up to him someday."

This piques my interest. "Who'd catch up to him?"

"The bookies, the other gamblers, I don't know. He had a problem and he owed a lot of people money. I warned him. I worried about him. Oh, God, murdered? Not my Jason."

"Paula, I'm so sorry to have to ask you these questions now, but is there anyone, in particular, that might have wanted to hurt Jason? Anyone that he was worried about?"

Paula gives a humph of derision. "Jason never worried about anything like he should. He didn't care who he owed money to or that we were broke. He just cared about the casinos, about the next poker game. I'm sure you men are familiar with gambling addiction. Well, Jason had it bad."

She looks around the room, holding the worn blue pillow close to her chest. "I'm gonna lose the house." She says the statement with such conviction. "We were already behind in the mortgage. He didn't make much at the car dealership, and what he did make he lost, but what am I going to do now?"

I wish I had answers for her. Wish I could soften the blow in some small way. Instead, I have to push for answers of my own. "Which dealership did he work at?"

Paula answers with a far-off look in her eye. "The Chevy dealer out on highway seven. He's been there for years, although he doesn't sell much. His buddy, David Benson owns the place.

They went to school together and I think David kept Jason on out of pity. Of maybe because Jason was bad at poker. They had a poker night every Friday, with David, Jason, and some other guys from work. Guess they'll have to find someone else to take advantage of now."

Paula sniffles as I jot all of this in my notebook.

"Who else played in these games?" Dustin asks. "You said other guys from Hartman College?"

She looks up suddenly. "How did you know he went to Hartman?"

"Tattoo on his leg," Dustin says. "I just guessed."

"Oh, that ugly thing. He hated that tattoo. Said he wished he could have it removed."

"The other poker players?" I gently prod her back to the question at hand.

She pushes her fingers against her forehead. "Oh, let's see. David, as I said. Brad Grady, Jonah Hopkins, sometimes this new guy played, Preston something, that works at the dealership."

That name hits close. Gabby's neighbor and ex-boyfriend Preston works at a car dealership.

"Did they play last night?"

"He said so. I saw him after I got home from work, then he headed out like he always does. I just assumed when he didn't come home that he took off somewhere with the guys. He's done it before." Her voice trails off. "How did he end up murdered? He was supposed to be losing half his paycheck to his buddies and coming home smelling like cigars."

"You've been very helpful, Paula. I'm sure we will have lots more questions later, but I think you've given us plenty to start on for now. Do you have someone you can call to come to be with you?"

She nods automatically. "My sister, Louise. You may want to talk to her. Jonah is her husband. No one else from the game is hurt are they?" Panic suddenly crosses her face. "This was supposed to be just between sisters, but Louise told me Jonah was getting sick of Jason and how he was throwing money around at the games. Acting like a big shot, even though Jonah knows we are broke. I guess a few times, Jonah lost on purpose so Jason would have some money left over at the end of the night. It was starting to cause tension, but Jason was clueless about it."

I look at Dustin and he reads my mind. We need to talk to Jonah Hopkins and fast.

Chapter 11

GABBY

The Charger rumbles to a stop in my driveway. I sit in the car, staring at my freshly painted garage door. It still hangs crooked, raised on the right a few inches. Beneath the fresh coat of white paint Lucas put on a few weeks ago, I can still see the faint remainder of words left by vandals over the years. FREAK, MURDERER, WITCH, and worse show through the white paint.

Or maybe it's just the memories of the words in my mind.

Either way, they sting.

Sticks and stones, and all that. But words *can* hurt.

I carefully turn away from my garage door and drag my tired body down the cracked sidewalk to my front step.

I itch at my left arm absently.

The peeling paint on my front door thankfully has no hurtful words scrawled in it. The vandals always choose to paint the garage. I slide my key into the lock with a jangle of metal keys.

My left arm stings.

I freeze, the key turned halfway, and listen to the universe.

"Gabby." I hear my name on the spring breeze. I look towards the sky, waiting for the rest of the message.

"I hate to bother you," the voice continues from my right. I blink at the sky and turn my head.

The voice isn't coming from the universe. It's coming from my neighbor and former boyfriend.

Preston.

Since we broke up several months ago, I have only seen him a few times when we've both been in our driveways at the same time. We've survived being neighbors by an unspoken agreement that we don't speak to each other.

Something must be wrong if he's come onto my property. I listen to my tattoo, hoping for some guidance, but my arm no longer stings.

I have to face Preston alone.

Stealing myself to be polite, I turn to face the man who I first trusted with my deepest secret. The man who tossed me aside immediately afterward.

"You're not bothering me. What can I do for you?" I use the tone of voice I perfected in my previous job as a catalog call-center order taker. Faked interest.

"I'm not sure." Preston looks everywhere except at me. "I think a guy I work with might be in trouble."

"Why's that?"

"Did you hear about that guy that was killed and found this morning?"

I nearly laugh out loud. I merely nod and say. "I heard about it."

"Well, he worked at the dealership. Quite a shock to all of us." He stares at the empty flowerbeds near my front step.

"I assure you that Lucas and Dustin are working the case to the full extent. There's nothing else to be done at this point." I reach for my keys still in the lock. "Unless you know something about Jason that will help the investigation?"

"I'm not worried about Jason. I mean, I am, but that's not why I came over here." He stammers, investigating the cracks in the concrete walkway with the toe of his shoe.

I don't want to be having any conversation with Preston. His beating around the bush is getting on my tired nerves.

"Why did you come then?"

"It's my boss, David Benson. He lives alone and basically lives to work." He says to the grass.

"Okay?" I prod.

"He's never missed a day of work in all the time I've been at the dealership. But today, he didn't come in. No one noticed at first, the news of Jason taking everyone by surprise, and all. I mean, I'm sure he's fine, but I have a bad feeling."

The man who dropped me like spoiled garbage when he found out about my "feelings" from my tattoo comes to me with a feeling of his own. How ironic.

I'm intrigued regardless.

"When did you last see him?"

"Last night at our poker game. We played at Brad's. Jason was there, too."

Any wisp of exhaustion floats away. "You played poker with Jason last night?"

Preston risks a look at me, then darts his eyes back to the grass. "Jason and David. Now Jason is dead and David is missing. I wanted to call the cops, but I thought it might be better if you told," he pauses, not saying Lucas's name. "The detectives." He finishes.

I already have my phone to my ear. Lucas answers on the first ring, and I explain the situation. "We'll be right there," Lucas says.

I slide the phone back in my pocket and look at Preston. "They'll be here in a few minutes."

The donut I ate earlier flips in my belly. My ex and my current boyfriend together at my house. This day just gets crazier and crazier.

We wait awkwardly. "So, how've you been?" Preston finally asks, toeing the concrete cracks again.

"I'm great. You?"

"Good. Real good."

That's as much small talk as I'm in the mood

for. "Wait here. I need to go inside for a minute."
I turn the key the other halfway and push through
my front door.

A gray and white blur darts at my feet, nearly
tripping me. I shove the door shut behind me and
bend to pet the cat. "Crap on a cracker, Chester, I
haven't been gone that long."

Except I have. It's been over twenty-four
hours since I left the house. I pick Chester up and
rub behind his ears. "Sorry, buddy. I know I
haven't been around much lately."

Chester purrs and rubs against me, forgiving
me. He then wiggles to be let down. His food dish
is empty and his water bowl is low. Keeping one
eye on the front window, I feed and water the cat,
then pour myself a glass of iced tea.

Preston wanders on the front walk, his hands
shoved deep in his pockets. He looks like a lost
child. I study his face, unconsciously comparing
him to Lucas. Lucas is tall and dark and fit.
Preston is smaller and lighter. His lips are thicker.
Lips I once kissed.

The thought makes the donut flip again in
distaste. Preston was a nice diversion, but he's
nothing compared to the man pulling to the curb

in front of my house.

Excited, I drain the rest of the tea and go back outside.

Preston seems small next to Lucas and Dustin dressed in full uniform with the vests under their shirts and the tools and guns on their belts. To his credit, he stands tall and reaches to Lucas first to shake hands. The men all shake and nod and then Dustin gets to the point.

"Gabby said you were with Jason Garafolo and David Benson last night. David never showed at work today?"

"That's right. I know it might seem like nothing, but with Jason," Preston swallows hard. "And then David not coming in. I feel like it has to be related."

"You might be right. What about Jonah Hopkins? He was at the game too?" Dustin asks.

"Yes. And Brad Grady. We all play every Friday. Last night we played at Brad's. Everything was normal. We played, then we left. Well, at least Jonah and I left. Jason and David were still there."

"Did Jonah seem upset when he left?" Lucas asks.

"Johan? No, he was fine. He even won last night. I broke about even as usual."

"How did Jason do?"

Preston looks across the yard, embarrassed. "I hate to talk bad about him, but he lost. He nearly always loses. He has no poker face. I wasn't really close to him, even though we worked together, but even I know he has a gambling problem. I always wondered why David let him play with us since the man had an addiction. You'd think his friends would try not to tempt him. David let Jason do whatever he wanted. Jason rarely sold a car, but he kept his job. I know they were college buddies and all, but I would have thought there would be a limit to the loyalty. I didn't go to college, so what do I know," Preston finishes with a shrug.

"You knew they went to Hartman College together. Did they talk about it a lot?" Lucas asks.

"Not at work so much, but at the games, Brad, David and Jason would get to reminiscing. Jonah and I got sick of it sometimes. That's why we left first last night. They were all talking about the good ol' days."

"Did David wear a ring?" I ask. "A red stone

in the center and colored stones around it. Kind of gaudy."

"Yeah, he and Jason and Brad all had them. Some club they were in together."

"Does Brad work at the dealership too?" Dustin asks.

"No. He's in financial planning at some firm in Fort Wayne."

"He lives in Fort Wayne?"

"No, here in River Bend. He's fourth generation in this town. Involved in the history and stuff. He's even on the board at the history museum."

Lucas, Dustin, and I all perk up at the mention of the museum. "The museum on the square?" I ask.

Preston nods. "Always bragging about how far back his family goes, how much stuff they've donated to the museum."

"Did you play poker at the museum last night?" I ask.

Preston seems confused. "No. We played at his house."

The four of us fall quiet, thinking about all Preston told us. Preston finally breaks the silence.

"So are you going to go check on David, make sure he's okay?"

"Of course we are. Don't worry. I'm sure he's fine. But we'll check it out and make sure." Lucas calms him.

Preston dares a look at me, "You'll let me know what they find out?"

"As soon as we know anything."

Preston shuffles his feet, "Well, if you don't have any more questions."

"We might later, but for now, I think we're good." Lucas reaches his hand out to shake Preston's again. I expect tension between the men, but they both seem more relaxed than when Lucas and Dustin first arrived.

"Thank you, Detective Hartley, McAllister." Preston nods to the men.

Preston gives me a grim smile, then heads back to his house.

"To David Benson's?" I ask once Preston is out of earshot.

Dustin looks at me with his familiar, 'you're not invited' look. "Come on. You wouldn't even have the lead if it weren't for me."

"Don't you think you should rest? You've

already done two visions today and you will be up late tonight at the museum." Dustin says, pretending brotherly love.

I glare at him. "You don't get to tell me when I need to rest, Brother. I'm a grown woman. And how do you know what time I'm going to the museum?"

"Mom called me." Dustin seems displeased. "Do you think it is a good idea to involve her in your schemes?"

Angry blood rushes to my face and heats my words. "Schemes? Is that what I do for a living? Was it a scheme that found you a dead body this morning?"

Lucas sighs audibly. "Please, you two, give it a rest. Dustin, we need to go check on David Benson. Gabby, sorry, but no you can't come."

He softens the words with a squeeze of my hand. "If there's something to his disappearance that you can help us with, you know I will ask. That reminds me." He pulls up a picture on his phone. "This is the tattoo Jason Garafolo has on his calf. Does it mean anything to you, or give you anything?"

I look at the picture of the horse head logo.

"Only that he liked his school. That's Hartman right?"

"Yeah. He also had the ring with the same logo." Lucas pushes the phone into my hand. "Can you get anything from a photo?"

Dustin sighs heavily, "I'll wait in the car."

I roll my eyes at my brother and remove my left glove. "I'll try." Closing my eyes, I say my usual prayer. "Lord, let me see what I need to see." I place my bare left hand over the screen of the phone and focus all my attention on the tattoo and the man whose leg bears it.

A faint image appears in my mind.

Young men in a circle. Someone talking in a loud whisper. Fear and panic. Guilt.

The image fades and I blink my eyes open and tell Lucas what I saw. "Some sort of meeting, maybe. Did Jason belong to a fraternity or anything?"

"I'm not sure. I'll have to ask his wife. Fear and guilt, interesting." Lucas muses. I expected something more like football games and parties. That sort of thing."

I pull my glove back on. "So did I, but I only see what I see."

134

He drops a kiss on my cheek, then pulls me to him. The strap of his vest pokes into my face. I wriggle into a more comfortable position. "When you're in uniform, you're like hugging a tank."

He lets me go mumbling, "Sorry."

I beam my best smile at him, "I'm not. I'll take hugging a tank over not hugging you at all."

Dustin honks the horn on the cruiser.

Lucas drops another quick kiss, this time on my lips. "You coming over tonight after you take your nap and then work at the museum?"

I warm at the invitation. "I was hoping you'd ask."

Chapter 12

GABBY

It rained while I napped and the air is full of humidity. By the time I reach my shop, my curls have frizzed in the damp, an almost physical sensation as each hair stretches. I dig an elastic hair tie out of my jacket pocket and attempt to tame the wild mass. The hair tie snaps in my fingers, the broken ends stinging through my thin gloves. Frustrated, I return to the Charger and search through the center console for another tie. My search comes up empty. I blow the hair out of my face and hope Mom has one at the apartment.

I feel eyes watching me in the back alley, the odd tickle at the base of my neck. I turn slowly from my car and search the dark alley. There's a pile of boxes Mom and Grandma left in the dumpster, the squares sticking out of the top. Other than that, the shapes of the alley are familiar and unthreatening. A light flicks on above me, and I see Mom at the window of the apartment, waving.

Feeling foolish for being frightened by an excited mother, I let myself in the back door of the shop.

Mom waits at the top of the stairs. "Ready for a ghost hunt?" she says.

"What are you wearing? You know we won't be sneaking into the museum. Mr. Trimble gave me the key."

Mom shrugs and smiles. "I know, but this is exciting." Mom is wearing what Grandma and I once affectionately called her ninja outfit. Black turtle neck, black jeans, her blonde hair tucked into a black hat.

"At least you aren't dressed as a Ghostbuster," I tease. "Do you have a hair tie? I broke mine."

"I don't know how you live with those curls," Mom muses as she enters the apartment. I follow and am once again enthralled with the pictures all over the walls. One of Dustin and me as kids makes me smile. "I'm glad you and Dustin are getting along better now. He told me you talked earlier today," I say.

Mom practically beams as she hands me a blue elastic. "It's like a miracle. One I owe to you."

I use the elastic and instantly feel more in control with my frizzed hair out of my face. "I don't cause miracles, Mom. God handles those."

Mom puts her palm on my cheek, then points to the scar on my eyebrow. "You and what you do are a miracle."

I grow uncomfortable under the direct praise. "Ready to go?"

"Do we need to bring anything?"

I hold up my left hand. "Have all the tools I need. Maybe bring your phone. We can use the flashlight if we need it."

Like an excited puppy, Mom practically dances with anticipation. "A real ghost hunt. Amazing. Do you think we'll see one?"

"I don't think there is a ghost, to be honest. But I've learned to keep an open mind."

"I wouldn't be too surprised. You should hear

all the noises this building makes at night. I know this is my first night here and you probably know better than I do, but I swear I heard footsteps earlier."

I search her face for the teasing smile, but she's serious. "An old building like this makes lots of sounds."

She shrugs one shoulder, uncomfortable. "I know that. This just sounded-." She stops in mid-sentence. "Maybe I'm just not used to being alone." A touch of sadness has crept into her voice.

"Mom, you know Grandma would love it if you stayed at the farm longer. You don't have to move out."

"I need my own space," she says, lifting her chin. "I'm fifty-two years old. I can't live with my mom."

"No one is judging you."

She humphs in disagreement. "Everyone judges me. For fifteen years I've been the woman that killed her husband and left her daughter to die. I may be out now, but some people never change their minds, never listen to the truth of a story."

In my exhilaration that the world finally knew for sure Mom was innocent and that she was back home with us, I never thought how it felt to her. "I know firsthand how narrow minded people in this town can be. I try to focus on the people that love me, not the people that judge me. You are innocent. You've always been innocent. Just focus on that."

Mom gives herself a mental shake. "Ghosts. I'd rather go search for ghosts." She turns on the heel of her black boot and leaves the apartment.

I press my face to the full-length glass door of the museum. Only a few well-hidden nightlights illuminate the interior, creating long fingers of shadow.

"Looks creepy in there at night," Mom says looking around her nervously. "This feels so wrong, like we're breaking in, or something."

I jingle the key on its bright green River Bend Historical Museum keychain. "Not breaking in. Invited guests." Mom glances in both directions down the sidewalk and around the town square. The courthouse looms like Indiana's answer to a gothic castle.

"Aren't you scared? Even a little bit?"

I grasp Mom's wrist and give it a reassuring squeeze. "You don't have to come with me if you don't want to."

She blows air at the bangs that have escaped her black hat. "I wouldn't miss it. I just get excited."

I slide the key into the lock and turn. It doesn't move. "Crap on a cracker," I mutter. "He better have given me the right key." I cup my face to the glass and look inside the dark building, hoping to see Gene Trimble waiting for us. He said he wouldn't be here, was too afraid to come this late at night.

"You sure you have the right key?"

"It's the only one on the key chain." The round green key chain hangs uselessly from the front door.

"Sometimes keys don't work on the first try," Mom says. "The key to my cell at the prison stuck all the time. Normally the doors are opened by electric circuits. If they needed to use the key for some reason it took a few tries."

My blood goes cold hearing Mom talk of prison. It's the first direct memory of her time there she has shared. The thought that she spent years in that horrid place still makes me sick. I visited her every month, and I know very well that she was there. I have a hard time reconciling the woman I visited in prison with the woman dressed as a cat burglar and wriggling the key in the lock right now.

I prefer the woman in black.

The key turns. "See." She beams triumphantly. "Now let's go find some ghosts."

She strides confidently into the dark museum, leaving me to hurry and catch up.

"So where do we start? Where does he think the ghosts are?" she whispers.

I whisper back, feeling foolish. "Slow down and let me do what I do. Okay?" I take off my gloves and shove them into my jacket pocket. "First I need to touch the things that have been moved, see what I can pick up."

Mom raises on her toes with excitement but keeps her mouth closed.

I first open my mind to the universe, close my eyes and say my prayer. "Lord, let me see what I need to see."

"Do you say that prayer every time?" Mom

whispers near my ear, making my eyes fly open.

I take a startled step away from her. "I need you to be quiet and just watch. Please. But yes, I say the prayer every time. Whatever this gift is, it comes from God. I always include Him in the visions. He shows me, tells me, what I need to know to help."

Mom nods like she understands. I get the feeling she truly does.

Feeling a little self-conscious with Mom watching me so intently, I first go to the candy dish display, the one Gene said had been moved. I pick up the larger of the dishes with my bare left hand and close my eyes again.

Uncertainty, indecision. Not worth it.

My eyes flutter open.

Mom's eyes are full of questions. I shake my head. The vision could mean anything, or nothing. It could be from the person who donated it to the museum in the first place. It certainly didn't feel like a ghostly presence.

I try the smaller of the carnival glass candy dishes. It is smaller in size, but more intricate and the colors are brighter.

I get nothing.

I rub the surface of the glass. It's rougher than I expected, not slick like the other dish. I reach deep into the history of the candy bowl, search for any scrap of an impression, anything at all.

The only thing I see is white, plain white like styrofoam.

The lack of history on a piece that should be at least a hundred years old finally makes sense.

"It's a fake," I tell Mom. "This one is real, but this one is a fake. I'm sure Gene would have known that when it was donated. Someone's changed it out."

She looks at my bare hand with wonder, then shakes her head. "Why would someone replace a candy dish with a fake?"

In answer, I hurry to the display of gold coins where Gene spotted the fake. "This coin is a fake, too. Gene is sure of it."

For good measure, I place my bare hand on the glass of the case, say my prayer, and close my eyes. It's a bit harder to sort out the impressions from the fake coin and block out the ones from the real ones so close. I'm satisfied with my findings and nod to Mom. "Replaced with a fake."

"The coin I understand. It has to be worth some money, but a candy dish?"

I shrug. "Maybe it's not worth the same as a gold coin, but I bet there's some value to it. Whoever took it first wanted the big one, but decided it wasn't worth it."

"So, no ghosts. Just a thief." Mom seems disappointed. She pulls the black hat off her head and runs her hands over her hair. "Not that I thought we'd see a ghost or anything."

I pat her on the shoulder. "Even better, we have a mystery to solve. Someone has been here. Gene even thought he saw someone. A blond in a white gown. Children laughing. Footsteps where there shouldn't be any."

"I heard footsteps earlier. You said it was just the old building."

"Probably is. He was sure he saw a woman, though." I chew on a fingernail in concentration. "And children."

On impulse, I find the marble collection with the missing Aggie. I hold my hand over the case. Instantly, images of children jump into my head.

Anticipation, desire, no I get to keep it, you got the doll.

146

"Have you seen a doll collection in here?" I ask.

We search the rooms and soon find an impressive display of dolls. Fancy silk dresses and elaborate hair do's fill shelves in a corner of one of the rooms. "Does it look like one is missing?"

I have a thing against dolls in general and the many eyes watching me in the dim light sends a shiver down my spine. Dolls, due to being handled so often, hold a lot of impressions. I don't want to open myself to them.

"There's a bit of a gap between these two."

"There's been kids here. Kids that have taken things."

"Like teenagers out for mischief?" I smile at her use of mischief.

"I get the sense they are younger. One took the Aggie one took a doll. That doesn't sound like teenagers. What would kids be doing in here late at night? And why would they take a candy dish and a gold coin?"

Out of the corner of my eye I see a display of pocket watches. There's a conspicuous gap in one of the rows. I hurry to the display and touch it.

Hurry, sounds, someone's coming.

"I think we interrupted them in the act here. They took the watch but didn't replace it."

Mom looks at the case. "Do you think it's the blond woman Gene saw? Or maybe there's a ghost and a thief?"

"You just really want a ghost don't you?"

"Well, a woman that disappears. What other explanation could there be?"

"I'm not sensing any ghosts or anything otherworldly."

"No offense, baby girl, but ghosts aren't your specialty."

"I'm the closest thing we have to a specialist in this."

"Then let's do this all the way. We have to be sure there're no ghosts."

"You want me to do a séance or something? That's not what I do."

"I'll help you. In prison, there wasn't anything to do except watch TV and I've seen a lot of those ghost hunter shows."

Mom leads me to the center of the museum. "Stand right here and open your hands. Maybe take off both gloves."

"Crap on a cracker, Mom. This is nuts."

"This is what he's paying you for."

Feeling like a circus sideshow, I do as I'm instructed. I hold out both my bare hands, palms up. To my surprise, my tattoo begins to tingle.

I might not follow this crazy idea of my mom's but I always follow what my tattoo tells me.

With hands out, I close my eyes and say my prayer. Almost instantly I sense someone in the room with us.

"There's someone here," I whisper to Mom.

"Holy crow, are you serious?"

"Shh."

I concentrate harder, trying to see more.

My tattoo is humming against my arm and I hear it.

Rare books.

"It's in the rare book room."

Chapter 13

GABBY

The door to the rare book room is closed but not locked. The handle on the door is the vintage kind with a glass knob. I nod to the handle and Mom understands. I don't want to touch it with my bare hand. A knob like that, touched by hundreds of people over decades of use would be full of impressions. As it is, the part of my mind that gets visions is starting to tire. I don't need to fill it with unneeded impressions.

Mom turns the handle and the door glides open.

The looming dark of the rare book room is deeper than the rest of the museum. The room has no windows and no lights on. The books are kept safe from fading and damage from light. I turn on the flashlight on my phone and scan the room. Under normal circumstances, I love books, would enjoy spending hours wandering through the few shelves.

Tonight is not the time.

I feel Mom's breath on my ear. "What's in here?"

The beam of my flashlight dips as I jump at her words. "Crap on a cracker, Mom. You nearly scared me to death."

"Sorry," she whispers, her hands on my shoulders as she cowers behind me. The room is deeply silent. A reverential silence that fits the books in the room. With my light held high, I start on the left side of the room, shuffling my feet across the wooden planks of the floor. The tallest of the shelves looms in the light of my phone, casting menacing shadows against the wall.

Hiding behind the shelving unit, I shine the light behind the shelf. I lean around the corner, so close to the shelf the unique smell of old books fills my nostrils. Mom leans with me, her hands still on my shoulders.

"Who's in here?" I call into the darkness behind the shelf. The light shines bright through the gloom, but the only thing it illuminates is a red upholstered reading chair at the end of the aisle.

"I don't see anything," Mom whispers in my ear again. My tattoo suddenly stabs my arm.

Hit the ground.

I obey instantly, pulling Mom under me.

A gunshot fills the room with sound, making my ears ring. The smell of gunpowder burns my nose.

Books fly from the shelf, bouncing off my back like raindrops of pain. The shelf teeters above us, dumping its load of priceless books but managing to stand upright.

Mom screams in terror and confusion below me.

"Are you hurt?" I shout at her in the dark, my phone and the light lost in the chaos.

"N-no," she stutters. "Holy crow, what was that?"

"That wasn't a ghost," I say, pushing out of the pile of books. I shuffle through the books looking for my phone. The light suddenly shines directly into my eyes, blinding me. Footsteps clatter across the wooden floor and the door slams.

"Come on," I shout to mom, knocking books off and helping her to her feet.

I run for the door, in my haste, forgetting about the old doorknob and my bare left hand.

The instant my fingers close on the glass knob, the images shoot through me.

Run is the strongest, most recent, from the person that shot at us, but a flood of images from the knob's past knocks the wind out of me. My fingers tighten on the knob and a flow of thoughts and memories crush through my mind.

Mom suddenly plows into me and the knob leaves my hand. I land on the floor, gasping for air, thrown by the power in such a small item.

"Gabby girl, are you okay?" Mom is at my side, her face illuminated by the beam of my phone that I once again dropped.

I fight for breath and to gain control of my thoughts. "I think so," I say quietly. "Holy crow." I use my Mom's favorite expression. "That was intense." I push off the floor and get to my wobbly legs.

"Someone was here."

"I know. They're probably long gone by now, but let's find out." I shine my light on the knob. "Will you do that for me? I'm never touching an old knob without gloves on again."

Mom turns the innocent looking knob and we escape the book room. "Which way do you think they went?"

I listen to the quiet of the museum. Footsteps pound on the second floor.

"Upstairs."

We run for the ornate stairway at the center of the museum and dart up the steps as fast as we can muster. The stupid doorknob visions sucked the energy out of me and I'm panting as we reach the top of the steps.

"Which way?" Mom asks, darting her eyes down both hallways.

A door slams above us. "I think they went into the attic. They're stuck now. I was there this morning and it leads nowhere."

We run down the hall towards the attic door. Mom obligingly opens the door, then stops me at the bottom of the steps. "What are we going to do once we find them?" Her voice is shaking, but I can't tell if it's from excitement or fear. "They have a gun."

"I don't know. I'm not good at planning ahead."

Mom looks around the hallway, spies a set of vases on a side table. She grabs them both, then hands me one. "I hope these aren't too valuable. We need weapons."

I've never seen this side of my mom before, but I like it.

I brace myself when she hands me the vase, but it only takes a moment for me to realize this, too, is a reproduction. I touch the one she holds with the tip of a finger and know hers is real.

"Another fake," I tell her.

"Well, whoever tried to hurt us is not fake." Mom starts up the stairs, leading.

The steps creak under us, loud and obtrusive as I strain to hear movement from the attic. On the street side of the attic, lights from the town center pour in. On the alley side, the room is dark.

As we reach the top of the steps, we peek over the floor, searching the shadows. The attic appears empty.

We take a few more steps, carefully scanning each corner of the room. A dressmaker's dummy startles me, and I make a small sound of fear.

"Just a dummy," Mom says, brave as can be. She has her phone out too, and scans the room, looking behind anything that could hide a person.

I close my eyes and sense the room. "I don't think anyone is here."

"Where could they go?" Mom asks confused. "Maybe they never came up here."

"They did. We heard the door open and shut and the footsteps pounding up the creaky steps."

Mom turns a complete circle. "If they're not here now...."

"A ghost didn't shoot at us then knock the books over." I interrupt.

"You don't know that. Ghosts can move things when they need to. I told you I've seen all the shows about it."

"Those shows are fake, Mom."

"Says the psychic."

"Touché."

We search the room again, to be sure no one is hiding and ready to pounce.

"The trunk that Jason Garafolo was found in was right here yesterday," I tell her. "I tried to sense what happened to it, but the trail was faint and just led to the wall. Most likely the trunk was over by the wall at one time and was moved here by the bed. I just got the vision wrong."

Mom drops to her knees and looks under the bed, even though it's too close to the floor to hide a person. She sits back on her heels and runs a hand over her bangs, leaving a dusty streak on her face.

I suddenly break out laughing.

"What's so funny?" She sounds a little hurt.

"This whole thing is funny. For years I dreamed of you coming home. Never, not once, did I dream you and I would be in a museum attic in the middle of the night searching for ghosts." I cross the room and throw my arms around her. "I love having you home."

Surprised and pleased, she returns the embrace.

"It certainly has been eventful." She squeezes me tight then let's go. "Now what? We didn't solve anything."

"We know someone has been taking real

items and replacing them with fakes. We know someone was here tonight."

"And then disappeared like a phantom, don't forget."

"Okay, I'll admit that is weird." I look around the room again. "Let me try something. I did it this morning, but I was focused on the trunk."

I'm feeling tired and spent so I sit on the bed before I start.

I open my hands wide and open my mind wider. "Lord, something is going on here. Please show me what I need to see."

I listen intently, expecting a tattoo tingle or a vision of some kind. Maybe see who the person was that tried to hurt us. Instead, I see the alley outside of my shop. I see my Charger parked near the dumpster. Pain wracks my body and I open my eyes.

"Anything?"

I shake my head, too disgusted with the false vision and to be wrong again to share what I saw with Mom.

"I think we've done all we can tonight. I'm not sure what I'll tell Gene tomorrow, but for now, I'm exhausted and hungry. The visions wear me out sometimes and I've done so many today my earlier nap didn't help much."

"Let's go back to the apartment. Your Grandma left some lasagna in the fridge for me and some tuna casserole."

My mouth waters thinking of the food waiting. "That sounds wonderful."

We lock up behind us and walk down the sidewalk to my shop. I let us in the front door, careful to lock up behind me.

My legs drag as I climb to the second-floor apartment. As soon as I enter what's Mom's now, I flop down on her couch. My eyes drift closed as she busies herself heating some food. Soon the little living room is full of the smell of lasagna cooking.

"I feel like I failed today," I mutter. "So many visions and none of them helpful."

"You saved Mr. Sickmiller and found a body that might have been missing for weeks." Mom soothes.

"If you say so."

I never get to eat the lasagna. I fall asleep before it finishes warming.

Chapter 14

LUCAS

My king size bed feels too big and too empty without Gabby next to me. I check the time again, wondering if she's done at the museum and headed this way. I don't want to text her and interrupt her investigation into the strange things at the museum. Whatever she finds may help with my own investigation into Jason's murder.

So far, it's the only real connection to anything we've been able to find. Except for the school connection.

After we left her house, Dustin and I went to check on David Benson, but no one answered the door and we had no cause to go inside. We did talk to a neighbor that was outside watering his flowers. He told us that Benson lived alone and he hadn't seen him. Figured he was at work.

Except he didn't go to work.

Next, we paid a visit to Brad Grady where the poker game was held. He had nothing useful. Yes, they played poker. Preston and Jonah left first, then Jason and David left together. Brad assumed they went home. He had no idea what happened to Jason or where David might be. Both Dustin and I got the feeling Brad was holding back on us, but we had nothing to push him on. Dissatisfied, we left.

Jonah Hopkins was much more open but had nothing helpful. He didn't hide his dislike of his brother-in-law, Jason, but he didn't hurt him. He came straight home from the poker game and his wife vouched for him.

Of the four men that spent the last hours of Jason Garafolo's life with him. Three men had nothing useful and one man is missing.

"David Benson left with Jason and now he's missing," I say to my bedroom ceiling for the tenth time. Saying it out loud doesn't make it lead anywhere.

I miss Gabby. If we could talk it over, I'm sure I'd put some of the pieces together. I check the time again. Just after midnight. I have no idea how long a museum "ghost" hunt takes, but I text her anyway.

A minute later, I get a response.

"This is Emily. Gabby's asleep on my couch. I'm going to have her stay here tonight."

I reply with a quick, "Ok." The short word hides my deep disappointment. I want her next to me, need her body with mine. I hold the pillow she slept on last night to my nose and smell the unique smell that is Gabby, a touch of coconut shampoo and something unnamable and lovely.

"Sleep well, Love," I tell the pillow. Then punching my pillow into shape, I curl on my side and will myself to sleep. I block all thoughts of the case from my mind and focus on Gabby. After half an hour, I give up. Like a lovesick teenager, I need her.

I think of calling, waking her. But I don't want to be so needy. I walk around my empty house, the case details plaguing me, swirling in my head.

I need Gabby.

The need overwhelms me, surprises me. We've spent nights apart before. I missed her then but survived just fine.

I finally give in and pull jeans and a t-shirt on. At the last minute, I strap my gun on. Since I've been with Gabby, I've learned to trust my instincts, to follow my gut.

My gut tells me to go to her.

My instincts tell me to bring my gun.

River Bend is quiet and dark at this time of night. Few cars are on the roads. It crosses my mind that I'm being ridiculous. It's nearly one in the morning. It's been a very long day and tomorrow will start early.

I don't turn around.

I don't call. I just drive.

The alley is dark and my headlights slice through the dim. My heart beats a little faster when I see her Charger. I park next to it and turn off my engine. I look out the windshield at the window of the apartment that overlooks the alley.

She's inside that window.

Feeling foolish, but resigned to the feeling, I climb out of my car. I have keys to the shop.

Something we exchanged a few months ago. The memory is sweet and the keys are useful. I slide the key into the back door, the other keys jingling softly.

Not loud enough to cover the moan of pain.

My body goes still, except for my right hand which instinctively goes for my gun.

My ears strain to hear the sound again. A low moan.

I leave the keys in the door and turn to the dark alley. To my right, the dumpster is overflowing with empty boxes. I pull my gun from its holster and put my back to the dumpster. I check both front and back, but there's nothing.

Ignoring the stench from the metal box, I round the corner and peer around the far side.

A body lies on its side, another low moan escapes the man.

I holster my gun and hurry to his side. He's barely conscious and bleeding from his head. I search for a pulse and find one, however unsteady and week. "Hang on, buddy," I tell the man. "I'm gonna get you some help."

His eyes flutter open and he mutters one word. "Sunny."

"Sorry man, it's the middle of the night. But you'll see the sun tomorrow."

I call dispatch and get an ambulance started as I keep pressure on the man's head wound. I then call up to Gabby. She answers on the fifth ring.

"Lucas?" she says sleepily. "I'm sorry. I think I fell asleep on Mom's couch." I can picture her looking around, her curls mussed from sleeping.

"I'm downstairs in your alley. I found a man hurt. Come down."

"My alley?"

"Yes. Just come down and help me."

"Crap on a cracker, I was right." She hangs up before I can ask what she was right about.

Chapter 15

GABBY

Lucas's call wakes me instantly. I push off the blanket Mom must have tucked around me, sprint down the stairs, and burst out the back door.

"Lucas, where are you?" I call into the dark. He responds from the far side of the dumpster. I hurry as fast as I can in my sock feet across the gravel strewn asphalt. I find him kneeling next to a man lying on his back, frighteningly still. "What happened? Is he okay?" I instantly feel foolish for the question. Of course, he's not okay.

"I just found him here. The ambulance is on its way." Lucas looks over his shoulder and gives me a wry smile. "I think he hit his head, maybe. His forehead is bleeding, but I can't find any other injuries." His voice is full of worry. "Where is that ambulance already?"

Far in the distance, sirens whisper on the night air. I join Lucas by the man. In my haste, I didn't put on gloves, so I keep my hands in my lap. A sense of déjà vu washes over me. I've been in this same place before. Recently. "It's my vision," I whisper. "I saw this exact view in my vision."

"Which vision?"

"Earlier, in the attic of the museum. I tried to get a sense of something, anything. This is all I saw, my car, the dumpster, the alley. I thought it was just a false vision. It must have been telling me this." I rub my arm, wondering why my tattoo didn't warn me that a man lay injured and possibly dying only feet from my back door.

Lucas watches me rub. "You had no way of knowing he was here."

"Didn't I?" I hold up my arm. "What is this for? What is all of this for?" I wave my arm, encompassing my shop.

"Gabby," Lucas says sharply, cutting through my growing hysteria. "You didn't do this to him. We don't even know what happened to him. You're here now."

You're being selfish. Stop moping.

I focus on the injured man. He hasn't moved since I arrived. His breathing is ragged and uneven. Lucas checks his pulse again. "Still there, but it's growing weaker." The ambulance sirens are growing closer, but are still a way off.

"Do we know who he is?"

"We pulled up David Benson's information after we talked to Preston. He looks like the ID photo in the system. I think we found the missing man." Lucas digs in the man's pocket for a wallet or ID. He doesn't find a wallet but pulls out an antique watch on a chain.

"Someone stole a watch similar to that from the museum. The watch and a bunch of other things. Looks like we found our thief." I hold my tongue about the gunshot. With the injured man next to us, now doesn't seem to be the time.

The slim moon glints on something on the man's hand. I take a closer look, careful not to touch. "Is that the same ring that Jason was wearing?" Lucas lifts the man's hand and inspects the ring. "It is. The horse head logo of Hartman College and all."

We look at each other. "Can't be a

coincidence."

Lucas holds the man's hand out to me. "Ambulance is only a minute or two away. Hurry." I mumble my prayer as I wrap my left hand around the man's.

The vision slams into me.

We didn't mean it, it was an accident, I'm not helping you anymore, let me go. Running, crashing, falling.

The ambulance lights glow against my closed eyes, interrupting the vision. "We need in," a voice shouts and I'm nudged away from the man by an EMT.

I scramble out of the way and stand near my car. Lucas joins me. "So?"

"He said something about an accident. Then I saw him running," I look up to the roof of my building, three stories away. "I think he fell from the roof."

Lucas follows my eyes. "Why was he on the roof?"

"I think he was running from someone."

"Gabby, what's going on? Are you okay?" Mom crashes out the back door. She's wearing a red nightgown with a cat on it. Her feet are bare, but runs across the gravel to me anyway and holds me close. "The ambulance isn't for me," I assure her. "Lucas found an injured man behind the dumpster."

Mom releases me and blinks against the bright lights of the ambulance, sleepy and confused. "I don't understand."

"I came to see Gabby and heard him moaning. Gabby thinks he might have fallen from the roof." Mom nods and accepts the odd situation without further questions. What kind of strange life we lead that a middle of the night finding of a nearly dead man doesn't faze her.

"Is he okay?"

"Not sure. He was breathing a minute ago, so that's something. He might have internal injuries if he fell that far." The activity behind the dumpster crescendos with shouts of, "He's crashing." The man is already on the gurney and the EMTs rush him to the back of the ambulance.

I take Lucas and Mom's hands and bow my head. "Lord, please let him be okay."

"Amen," Mom adds for me. I don't let go of their hands, just pull them closer to me as the ambulance speeds away.

The alley feels emptier and darker after all the excitement. My heart feels the same. "I should have known he was here," I whisper. "If I'd found him sooner, he might have been safe."

"You will not blame yourself for this," Lucas states firmly. His gaze shifts to the roof. "Do you know how to get to the roof?"

"I know there's a door to the third floor on the landing that goes to the apartment, but I've never gone up there. Maybe Grandma knows. She owns the shop."

"I hate to wake her. Show me the door." Lucas opens the back door and holds it for Mom and me.

"Is Dustin coming?" Mom asks as she passes him. The note of hope in her voice stings my heart.

"I wasn't going to bother him until I knew what we were dealing with." Lucas flicks his eyes at me and we share a moment of concern. Both of us have noticed the tension that seems to be building at home for Dustin. A middle-of-the-night call might not be what he needs right now.

The three of us crowd the landing. "Emily, why don't you go into the apartment." He unlatches the snap on his gun holster. "Gabby, I don't suppose you could stay here with her?"

"You know better than to believe that. Wait." I hurry into the apartment and grab a knife out of the new knife block Grandma and Mom bought this morning. "Ready."

"If you need to carry a knife, maybe you shouldn't go with him." Mom's voice rises an octave with worry. "Stay here with me."

I pat Mom's shoulder. "Don't worry. I'll be fine. Lucas would never let anything happen to me."

"I still think you should wait for Dustin."

"We don't even know if there's a reason to worry. We're just going to take a quick look around on the roof if we can even get up there from here."

Mom tugs at the hem of her nightgown making the smiling cat with the coffee cup dance.

"If you're so sure there isn't danger, then I'm going with you. I will not wait here while my daughter goes into something where she can get hurt." She raises her eyes to challenge first me, then Lucas.

"I see where Gabby gets her stubborn streak

from," Lucas says.

Both Mom and I slap him playfully on the arm. "You better believe it, buddy," Mom says.

"Just let me grab some shorts." Mom disappears into the bedroom and returns a minute later still wearing the cat nightgown, but now with jean shorts underneath. The outfit is about as far from the all black cat burglar/ninja get up she had on before. She selects her own knife from the block and beams at me.

"Let's go find some bad guys."

"This isn't a movie, Mom."

"Besides whoever might have chased the man off the roof was most likely long gone before I even got here."

Our unusual trio crowds the landing and Lucas and Mom look at me. "What?"

"The key."

"Is it locked? I've never even tried the door."

I still haven't put gloves on and there's no way I'm touching the old handle after what happened earlier.

Lucas does the honors and the unlocked door opens quietly. A rush of hot, stale air fills the landing. Lucas reaches for a switch and the stairway fills will pale light from a single bulb way up high.

I start up the steps, and Lucas gently pulls me back. "Excuse me, darling. I'm the cop, the one with the gun. I'll go first."

I step aside and let him lead. Mom crowds close behind me, whispering. "What do you think is up here?"

"Knowing Grandma, I'd assume she stored some stuff up here years ago and forgot all about it."

Lucas turns and puts his finger to his lips to quiet us. I shrug an apology.

The third floor looks much like the attic at the museum. Unfinished walls. A line of windows that overlook the street side, wooden walls. As I figured, there's a bunch of old beauty shop equipment stored here. Stuff Grandma used in her shop, no longer needed and couldn't bear to part with. Three ancient bubble-head dryers are lined up against one wall.

"I remember these from when I was a kid," Mom says full of nostalgia. She runs a finger over the fake gold trim of one of the headcovers. "I used to think this was real gold, turns out it's just paint."

The single light bulb does little to illuminate the corners of the room. With the flashlight on my phone in one hand and the knife in the other, I search for a way up to the roof. "What are we looking for? Stairs, a ladder? Any ideas?" I ask Lucas.

He shines his phone light around and has no answer to offer.

Besides a thick coat of dust on everything, there isn't much to see. The entire third floor was probably one long room back when this building was an auto parts manufacturer, but it has long since been divided into individual shops. Grandma owns from wall to wall and all three floors, but that's it. The museum owns their section, the empty antique boutique next door must own theirs. The clothing store between my shop and the donut shop must own theirs. Of course, the donut shop would have its own attic.

I imagine they all look like this. Rough wood, a bank of windows, and some discarded items.

"How did the man get to the roof if that's where he fell from? Maybe from one of the other stores?"

"If these attic spaces were all one room back in the day, maybe the roof access is in one of the others," Mom offers.

"I have an idea," I walk to the closest wall and touch the old wood with the bare tip of my left pointer finger. "Maybe I can find a door or something."

"Worth a try," Lucas says. I can't help feel a surge of thankfulness that he just agrees, that he believes I can be helpful. Better than having to fight with Dustin at every other scene.

As if thinking of my brother summoned his presence, he bellows up the stairs and heavy footsteps thump on the old wood. "Hartley, what the hell?" he demands.

"We're up here," Lucas replies needlessly. Dustin stomps up the last steps, his angry face rising into view.

"Why in the world do you have my mother and my sister up here on an investigation?"

Chapter 16

DUSTIN

A car drives through my neighborhood, casting shifting shadows across the walls of my bedroom. Sleep alludes me. Details of the case sift through my mind, driving away chances of rest. Next to me in bed, Alexis turns in her sleep, her hand landing next to mine on top of the bedspread. I link my fingers through hers, stealing a moment of contact while she sleeps on.

"I love you," I whisper so low I know it won't wake her. She squeezes my hand in her sleep and my heart swells.

It's the most intimate contact we've had for weeks.

Details of the case of my fizzling marriage might destroy me, so I push them from my mind.

With a mumble, Alexis releases my hand and turns away from me. I remind myself that she's asleep, that she doesn't mean anything by the action.

It still stings.

Giving up on sleep, I drag my tired body to sit on the edge of the bed. I rub at my shoulder, still sore and aching. The months of rehab have restored my range of motion to almost normal, but have done little to alleviate the bone-deep pain from the gunshot.

No amount of rehab will dispel the betrayal from my father. No amount of police department-required therapy has helped with the terror of facing my death.

I sigh heavily and walk out of the bedroom. Across the hall, I peek in on Walker. He's sound asleep in his new "big boy" red sports car bed. I have the sudden urge to touch him, to reassure myself he's safe. His warm hair caresses my palm. I drink in the feel of him. Drop a kiss on his head and breathe deeply of his little boy scent. In his sleep, he bats an arm at me, pushing me away.

I chuckle low in my throat. Even my son doesn't want my touch tonight.

I leave him to his sleep and wander the house.

More shifting shadows slide across the kitchen walls as I get a drink of water and stare into the front yard. It's too dark to see, but I know the grass needs cut.

Maybe tomorrow. If I can find the time.

I rub a hand down my face, tired to the core, yet knowing sleep will not come.

The ringing of my phone tears through the dark house. The ring tone for dispatch. I left my phone on the nightstand and run to stop the uncannily loud noise.

Alexis is wide awake when I reach the bedroom. She recognizes the ring tone and wears the irritated face I've seen so often lately.

"Duty calls," she says. She punches her pillow, too hard, and turns her back to me.

I punch the screen to answer the call. "McAllister."

Regina from dispatch says, "I hope I didn't wake you, Detective."

I look at the clock, it's past one, does she think I never sleep?

With a longing look at Alexis, I leave the bedroom and shut the door behind me. "I was awake. What's the problem?"

"Detective Hartley called for an ambulance a short time ago. He found an injured man in the alley behind your sister's shop."

The hollow feeling in my belly grows.

Gabby. That's all I need tonight.

Regina continues. "He didn't ask for you, but I thought you should know. The ambulance has already been sent and Detective Hartley is the only one on scene at the moment."

I rub my hand over my face again and blow air in exasperation. "Thanks for letting me know, Regina."

Pride and importance fill her voice as she says, "You're welcome, Detective. Just call and let me know if you need more officers on scene or anything."

"I will. Thanks again."

I hang up on Regina as anger simmers in my chest. Lucas should have called me. I'm his partner for heaven's sake. I don't understand where his mind goes where Gabby is concerned. It's like she has some spell on him that makes him forget procedures. She has some spell on everyone, always gets what she wants.

I clench my jaw in anger and creep back into my bedroom for clothes.

I expect Alexis to roll over and ask me where I'm going, ask for details, or at least show some interest.

I'm disappointed by my wife again. I can tell by her breathing that she's awake, but she keeps her back to me.

After dressing and putting on my gun and badge, I stand and stare at her back.

"I've been called on a case," I finally say.

"I know that." She doesn't roll over.

"Sorry, the phone woke you." I try.

"I'm used to it."

One long strand of her hair is spread across the bed like it's reaching towards me. I long to touch that strand, to run my fingers across its silky surface. I want my wife back.

Not long ago, she would have gotten up with me, made me some coffee, kissed me goodbye, and wished me luck.

The woman in my bed now is a stranger compared to the woman she was just a few months ago. The change doesn't make sense to me.

The greatest case of my life and I can't solve it.

"Alexis?" I'm not sure what word will come next, I just need her to look at me.

Surprisingly, she obliges.

She rolls over. In the dim light of the bedroom, her face looks pinched and pained. "I'm sorry I have to work."

"That's fine. They need you."

I need you.

"I don't know when I'll be back."

"I know that. Walker and I will be fine." She tries to keep the accusation from her tone but fails. The unspoken words, the insinuation that work is more important to me than family is clear.

"You know I'd rather be here."

"That's what you say."

"Alexis, what the hell is going on?" My brain tells me to stop talking. My mouth has other plans. "You act like I've done something wrong. What have I done? Worked hard for this family? Is that my crime?"

She blinks slowly, her mouth scrunching, her brain forming a response. "This isn't about you."

"Then what is it about? I'm sick of pretending everything is okay with us when obviously, it's not."

"I'm just going through some things. I don't want to talk about it." She pulls the covers over her protectively. "Go save the world. We'll be here when you are done."

She says the words quietly, but they feel like a slap.

"Alexis, please, talk to me." I hate the note of pleading in my voice.

She rolls over, away.

Her hair is tucked under the blanket now. No part of her reaches for me.

Exasperated, I leave the bedroom, leave the house.

I focus my anger away from home, away from my wife.

Drumming my fingers on the steering wheel, I drive too fast to Gabby's shop and park in the back, in the alley.

I expect to see other officers on the scene, but the alley is dark. Lucas's car is parked next to

Gabby's Charger. Mom's new little white car is parked next to Gabby's.

"A middle of the night family party," I mumble angrily.

I slam the door of the car too hard, then hurry to the back door of Gabby's shop. I don't knock, just let myself in. Up the stairs, I hear talking. Mom and Gabby and Lucas discussing something, probably about the hurt man that was found.

Even blocked out from the case.

I take the stairs two at a time, banging my way up to the third floor. No one hears me, they're too involved in talking to each other.

"Hartley, what the hell?" I demand. "Why in the world do you have my mother and my sister up here on an investigation?"

Chapter 17

GABBY

Mom and I have very different reactions to Dustin's sudden appearance.

Anger flushes through me.

Mom gushes. "Dustin, you're here. I told them we should call you."

Dustin levels his gaze directly at Lucas. "You should have called me. Or at least called someone."

Lucas straightens his shoulders and faces Dustin. "I was going to call you if there was a need. It is the middle of the night and I thought you'd rather be home with your family than chasing a ghost."

"I don't need you to think for me. Let me

worry about when I should be with my family." His words are clipped. A tone he often uses with me, but I've never heard him use with Lucas before.

I don't like it.

"Don't come barging into my place and snap at everyone."

Dustin glares and I can tell he wants to say more. He shifts his eyes to mom's smiling face and back to me. I remember the look from when we were kids and the unspoken promise of "this isn't over."

Mom is oblivious to the tension, she's just happy to see him, happy to be part of all of this. "We're looking for a way to get on the roof. Gabby thinks the man that got hurt might have fallen."

"He was chased," I say with certainty that I don't truly feel.

"If he was chased off the roof, then the person might still be up here. This is way too dangerous," Dustin fumes at Lucas.

"You try to stop them," he replies.

"It was at least an hour or so ago when we got shot at. Whoever did that probably chased that man off the roof, too. Then took off." Mom says the words so matter-of-factly, it's a little creepy. If getting shot at doesn't shake her up, I can't imagine what she must have lived through in prison.

"Shot at!" Dustin and Lucas exclaim at the same time. Identical looks of shock and anger are directed at me.

"You didn't think to call me about that?" Lucas asks. "Or at least call 9-1-1."

"Where were you when this happened?" Dustin talks over him.

My face burns with a mixture of guilt and indignation. "We were at the museum looking into the moved and missing things. Gene Trimble's ghost. I'm happy to report there is no ghost, but someone has been taking things and replacing them with fakes."

"You are evading the question." Lucas sounds so angry, I barely recognize his voice. "Shot at?"

"Not shot at, just shot near. I got a sense that someone was in the rare books room. We went to check it out and someone shot a gun near us then knocked a bookcase over on us."

Mom joins in, "Then we chased whoever it was up to the third floor, but they disappeared. Gabby says it wasn't a ghost, but where did the person go?"

"Ghosts don't carry guns," Dustin says, rubbing his face in exasperation. "What were you thinking not calling that in?"

"I was thinking that we were fine. They didn't shoot to hit us, just to scare us. Then they were long gone, so what could you have done. Besides when I tried to sense where they went or who they were, all I saw was my car and the dumpster. I must have been channeling David Benson. He had the missing watch in his pocket. He must have been at the museum tonight."

"But he didn't have a gun on him." Dustin's voice is deceptively calm.

"Maybe he ditched it somewhere." I'm grasping and know it.

"You said he was being chased off the roof," Mom points out. "Oh no, you don't think he was running from us when he fell do you?"

I search my vision. My memory of the sensation is fuzzy. "Running and falling I remember. But there was more to it."

"So let me get this straight," Dustin says, his eyes pinning me. I feel like a suspect being interrogated, complete with the single light bulb hanging from the ceiling. "You and mom go ghost hunting at the museum. You determine someone is stealing. You then get shot 'near' and chase after the person who then disappears at the same place where the trunk was that had a dead body in it this morning." He paces in his agitation, rubbing his hand over his hair. "You then not only don't call your boyfriend or your brother or the police at all, but you go to sleep?"

He stops pacing and stands very close to me. "Even for you, Gabby, that's pretty irresponsible. You force all of us to trust your visions, but you didn't even follow up on yours and check out the alley."

I square my shoulders and face down my brother. "I had no idea he was out there hurt."

"You knew someone dangerous was around with a gun." He leans so close to my face, I can see the red lines in the whites of his eyes. "It's bad enough that you put yourself in danger, but you put Mom at risk, too."

"That's enough, man," Lucas intervenes.

"Is it? I don't think so. She has to learn her actions affect others." Dustin then faces Lucas with similar venom. "What if you found the person that shot at them up here?" He points to the knife in my hand. "A knife in a gun fight? Seriously? What spell does she have you under?"

"Dustin," Mom says his name the way only a mother can. "Stop this."

Dustin seems to come back to himself. He shifts his eyes from Mom, to me, to Lucas then back to Mom. His shoulders finally slump.

"You guys do what you want," he turns and starts down the steps. "I'm calling this in and we'll search the roof and the museum and whatever else we need to search." He stops three steps down and looks at Lucas. "This is a police matter. Are you coming?"

Lucas looks at me, his expression clouded with confusion. "Maybe he's right."

The words sting more than they should. Of course, he's right, but I'm not going to admit it now. "Go."

"Are you coming down?" he asks.

I feel trapped and wish I could do the whole night over. Mom puts her hand on my back.

"Come on, Gabby girl, let's leave this for the police."

I look around the dusty room and the old beauty shop equipment. Lots of dust, but no door to the rest of the building or the roof. "I suppose there's nothing else to be found up here." I follow Lucas down the stairs with Mom right behind me. Dustin is long gone.

"You'll tell me what you find out, right?" I ask Lucas once we're back in Mom's apartment and I've returned the knife to the block.

Lucas gives me an exasperated and exhausted look. "Let's just see what happens."

I finger the necklace he gave me for Christmas nervously, half afraid he means with our relationship, not with the case.

"Stop worrying. He'll come back around. He always does," he says.

I'm not ready to admit Dustin is right and I don't want to talk about him.

"Keep an eye on him, please," Mom says. "Something more than tonight's events is bothering him. He might be prickly, but he needs us."

Lucas makes a small sound of laughter.

"Prickly is a good way to explain him. No worries, Emily, he's my partner and my best friend."

Mom seems relieved. I'm irritated and jealous. I want to throw myself into his arms, force him to tell me everything is okay. I settle for the small smile he gives me before he leaves.

"Lock this door behind me," he says, then he's gone.

The apartment feels empty without him. I finger my necklace again.

"Stop looking so beaten," Mom says. "That man loves you. He's not upset with you right now, he's upset with himself."

"Because he did what I wanted, not what he should."

"That was his decision to make." Mom takes me into her arms. I melt into the embrace. She gives a small laugh. "You sure upset our brother tonight."

I push away and wipe at my face. "Yeah, we fight a lot lately."

"You two fought all the time as kids, too. I think some siblings are just like that. You have to remember it comes from a place of love. That's what this whole mess tonight was about. He worries about you, and me."

"Haven't I proven I can take care of myself? Getting shot near and having some books fall on me is about the tamest thing to happen to me in a long time."

"That doesn't mean the people who love you won't worry."

I'm growing uncomfortable with the conversation. "Can we talk about something else? Like why was David Benson here tonight and is he the one that shot at us. If he was, then is he also the one that shot Jason Garafalo?"

Mom shakes her head in gentle exasperation. "Oh, Gabby girl, do you ever stop?"

"Sometimes," I hedge. I glance at the clock on the wall and see it's past two. It's been less than twenty-four hours since I found Mr. Sickmiller and the box in the ditch. "I suppose a lot has happened today. Maybe it can wait until tomorrow."

"Let Dustin and Lucas take care of it. That's their job." Mom attempts to stifle a yawn and fails. "I'm tired. Are you going to sleep here?"

I'm exhausted but too keyed up to sleep yet.

"If I stay here, I'll only want to go see what they're doing down at the museum, or if they find a way to the roof. Besides, Chester has been neglected the last few days." I give Mom a quick hug. "Thanks for coming with me tonight. Sorry I put you in danger."

"You don't make decisions for me," she says. "I practically begged to come. Not your fault that man was there with a gun."

I'm still not sure David Benson was the one who shot at us, but it's as good a theory as any.

"You sure you want to stay here tonight? Grandma Dot won't mind if you go to the farm."

"With the police all over the block, I couldn't be safer." She stifles another yawn.

"Sure has been an eventful first night for you."

"Better than night after night of boredom like I'm used to."

"Who ever thought life in River Bend could be so exciting?" I hug her again and repeat Lucas's "Lock this door behind me."

As I make my way down the steps, I hear the lock click into place. Feeling satisfied that Mom is safe, I lock the back door behind me. In the alley, I stand in the place where David Benson was found. I look up at the roof. The stonework is crumbled a bit directly above me.

"Were you running from us or someone else?" I ask the alley.

The alley doesn't answer.

Chapter 18

GABBY

Chester is indeed pleased to see me come home and sleeps next to me all night. I wrap my arms around him, wishing I was at Lucas's house in his bed, in his arms instead. I sleep the fitful sleep of one who knows she's done something wrong but has no way to fix it.

I drag myself away from Chester in the morning, and mentally prepare for my meeting with Gene Trimble. We have plans to meet as soon as the museum opens today to talk about his ghost problem.

The back alley is blocked with crime scene tape so I must park in front of my building. I don't want to see the place where Lucas found David Benson. I still have not heard from Lucas and gotten any update on what they've found out. The crime scene tape in the alley is a bad sign. If they thought David had an accident, the tape wouldn't be necessary.

Down the block, Lucas and Dustin's cruiser is parked near the museum door. As much as I want to see Lucas, I have no interest in dealing with Dustin this early in the morning. Considering that he's most likely been up working all night, I'm sure he's in an even grumpier mood than he was several hours ago.

I'm itching to know what they found out, if anything. I watch the door of the museum from my car, willing it to open and Lucas to appear. He might be coerced into telling me something.

The smell of fresh baked goods wafts in the open window of my car as I wait, giving me an idea for a peace offering.

The heavenly smell of donuts and frosting envelops me as I enter the bakery. Mitzie is behind the counter and rushes to greet me.

"Gabby, do you know what's going on out there? The cops were down the block when I got here this morning and there's crime tape in the alley."

I'm not sure how much to tell her. For once, I opt to keep my mouth shut. "I'm not sure."

"Do you think it has something to do with the dead man found yesterday?"

I blink in surprise, thinking she's talking about David Benson and wondering how she knows he's dead and not just hurt. "Dead man?"

Mitzie continues, excitedly, "I saw you on the news talking about it. You seriously found a dead man in a box? You live such an exciting life."

"Not really." I study the donut display more intensely than necessary. "Can I get some to go, please?"

"Gonna take them to that detective?" she asks with a sly smile. "I saw him and your brother milling about down there earlier."

"Cops and donuts, right?"

Mitzie checks over her shoulder to make sure her employees can't hear her and leans close. "If there's any way they could spare a minute, I wanted to make a report."

"I can't promise anything. They are pretty busy, I'm sure," I say, but my curiosity is piqued.

She glances around the empty store nervously. "It's a silly thing, really." She rubs her hands together, brushing stray flour off of the back of one of them. "I had a box of yesterday's unsold donuts over there on the counter when I left. This morning, the box was almost empty. I'm sure there were at least two dozen donuts in it, now there are only four. I counted them out because I sell them discounted, you see." Mitzie continues to rub her hands together although there's no flour left on them.

"Stolen donuts?"

"I know it's a tiny thing and not really a police matter." She glances toward the kitchen again. "See, this isn't the first time product has gone missing. It's never anything big. A loaf of raisin bread one time, some muffins another." Mitzie sights in agitation. "I thought maybe one of my employees was taking them, but I know that no one was here between when I left yesterday and when I opened this morning. The donuts were just gone. It's like a ghost is taking things." She laughs nervously.

"I don't think ghosts like raisin bread," I say, trying a joke to make her feel better. "I'll tell

Lucas about this. If someone is breaking in and stealing from you, it is a police matter."

Mitzie sighs with relief. "Thank you. I knew you'd understand." She looks pointedly at my gloved hands. "I don't suppose you sense anything, do you? Does your gift work that way?"

I shove my hands into my pockets. "It doesn't work like that."

Mitzie's shoulders drop in disappointment and she makes a soft "oh" sound. "Well, it was worth a shot. I should invest in security cameras, but I honestly never thought I'd need them." She takes a breath. "Now, what can I get for you?"

I order a selection of donuts to take to Lucas and whoever else is down there and leave Mitzie to her mysterious disappearing baked goods. Her story is eerily too similar to Gene's.

I sit the box of donuts on the roof of my car, slip off my right glove, and take a cream-filled one for myself. I stand on the curb, relishing the soft deliciousness, staring at the museum door and the green logo on the front, stealing my nerve to walk down the block and worm my way in with the box of goodies.

I do have an appointment with Gene this morning, so it's not like I'm just butting in. I doubt that Gene even remembers his concerns with the moved items and his "ghost" with the police once again in his museum.

Swallowing the last of my donut, I feel much braver with the sugar rushing my system. I lick the last bit of frosting from my fingers, put my glove back on and close the donut box. With my chin held high, I carry the box down the block.

The inside of the museum is cool and dark. Mable is at her post at the front desk, her head turned, staring at Lucas who's talking to Gene across the lobby. She recognizes me and instantly looks to her desk, suddenly very busy with some pretend paperwork.

I only have eyes for Lucas, but his expression is hard to read.

"I have an appointment with Mr. Trimble this morning," I explain. I hold up the box, "And I brought donuts."

Gene rushes to me. "Heavens, heavens, Gabby. I can't believe you were shot at last night." He seems like he wants to hug me. I make sure to keep the box of donuts between us so he can't. He settles for an awkward pat on my shoulder.

"It's okay, Mr. Trimble. The good thing is there's no ghost." I flick my eyes to Lucas. "Donut?"

He hesitates, and I worry he's still upset with me. I give him a tentative smile and he finally relents. "I'd love one. Thank you." He takes the box from me, purposely touching my hand in the process. His finger brushing against my gloved one feels like coming home and the knot that had been in my stomach since he left last night loosens.

Lucas sits the box on Mable's counter and offers her one. The older woman blushes prettily, but declines.

"Just awful, awful," Gene says, stepping even closer. "That poor man that died in our alley. I just can't believe it." I flash my eyes to Lucas for confirmation.

"Died?"

He nods once.

A mix of feelings rushes into me. If he was the one that shot at Mom and me, it's hard to mourn too much at his passing, but a loss of life is always sad.

"Did you find the gun yet?"

"Not yet. We've been all over the museum and the attic area. We've covered the businesses between here and your shop to be sure," Lucas says. "The roof access is from the attic area of the clothing store. There's a small staircase there. How he got from the museum to that staircase is a mystery." He raises his eyebrows in question and glances at my hands.

Mr. Trimble grows excited. "Maybe you can figure it out, Gabby. Mysteries are your forte, right?"

I shake my head vigorously. "I already tried last night. I didn't get anything." I have no interest in further failure today.

"Hey, Dustin, Gabby brought donuts," Lucas calls suddenly, his attention focused behind me. A new knot twists in my belly. I paste on a smile and turn to face my brother. He looks tired and worn. A niggle of worry joins the knot.

Dustin looks at the box, hesitates for a short moment, then helps himself. He mumbles a thank you around a mouthful.

Donuts must be magic if Dustin actually told

me thank you. Or maybe it's just that we have strangers around and Grandma Dot drummed manners into us.

"Do you have any confirmation whether David Benson was involved in Jason's murder?" I ask Lucas. He shakes his head in a way that tells me to ask again later when we don't have extra ears listening. I change tactics. "Gene, if these detectives are done with you, I'd love to go over what I found out last night."

"Right, right." He takes off his glasses, wipes them, then puts them back on. "Is that okay, Detectives?"

"I think we have what we need for now. We might have a few more questions later," Dustin wipes frosting from his lip.

"We can talk in my office." I follow Gene to a small room behind Mable's counter. I'd forgotten the woman was there, but she's obviously watched and listened to every word closely. I can imagine she's hoarding details to share with her friends later.

Gene settles into a dark red padded chair and I take the chair opposite the massive oak antique desk. I imagine if I touched the piece of furniture it would have some stories to tell. I cross my arms and tuck my hands away.

"First thing is good news. I don't think you have a ghost. I didn't pick up any vibes from one, at least." I have no idea what vibes from a ghost would feel like as I'm not sure ghosts exist, but Gene seems relieved.

"That's good, good." He leans back in his chair. "What's the other news?"

"Someone is stealing from you."

He sits up in surprise. "Stealing? I was afraid of that?" He fiddles with some papers on his desk. "To be honest, I'd prefer a ghost. Do you know who it is?"

"I think it is the man that fell off the roof. He apparently shot at us last night and he had the watch I noticed was missing in his pocket. Looks like he was taking things and replacing them with fakes."

"How? I lock up every night."

"Do board members have keys?"

He slides the papers on his desk around. "I think so. Do you think a board member is involved?"

"Brad Grady played poker with David

Benson the other night. He's on the board here, isn't he? Some sort of big shot?"

"His family is a major donor if that's what you mean. That trunk that you found was one of their donations, come to think of it. Yes, Brad Grady might have a key, probably does."

"If Brad and David are friends, Brad could have given him the key, or David might have taken it from his house somehow."

"I suppose so. I can't see Brad being involved on purpose. Why donate things if you're just going to steal them back? Why steal anything from here in the first place? The things that are missing are not super valuable. I mean, maybe several hundred dollars all together. A man like David or Brad makes more than that in a day or two."

I agree with Gene that the robberies don't make sense. Nothing about the two deaths makes sense.

Jason was obviously shot and David accidentally fell.

Or was chased?

I look at my gloved hands, angry that I didn't get more information.

"Thank you for everything you did for me last night," he says, opening a drawer and taking out a bank bag. "I'm so sorry that you almost got hurt. Even sorrier that poor man fell to his death. He may not have been nice, shooting at you and stealing, but still."

"I know what you mean."

Gene counts out some bills on the massive desk then hands them to me. I hesitate to take my payment after all that has happened. I then remember the unpaid electric bill hanging on my nearly empty fridge at home. I pocket the money.

"Another thing I don't understand," Gene says. "If David was the one behind the missing and moved items, and there is no ghost here, what or who did I see that day? The blond woman in the white dress."

Chapter 19

GABBY

I catch a glimpse of Lucas's back just slipping out the front door of the museum as I exit Gene's office.

"Lucas, wait!"

He stops, holding the door open for me. "I stalled Dustin as long as I could," he explains. "But Gomez has some information for us on David Benson."

"No worries." I smile as prettily as I can, meeting his eyes. I even flutter my eyelashes the way Grandma Dot once showed me in high school. "Don't suppose there's room for me in that conversation is there?"

Lucas laughs out loud at my attempt. "You know Gomez would have my head if I brought you to an autopsy report." He walks backward down the sidewalk, towards the waiting cruiser, away from me. "I like that eyelash thing you just did. Try it again tonight at my house?" The spring sun glints off his blue, sparkling eyes.

I can't help but beam back at him, even though I'm disappointed about not going to the coroner's.

I kiss my fingertips in goodbye and watch him drive away. Only after they turn the corner at the end of the block, do I remember about Mitzie and the missing donuts. Making a mental note to tell him later, I stand on the sidewalk and soak in the warmth of the sun. Closing my eyes, I tip my head back and let the brightness soak through.

A tingle at my tattoo interrupts my moment of connection to nature.

Look right.

As always, I obey without question.

I open my eyes and look across the square, past the courthouse, to the sidewalk opposite mine.

A familiar woman walks quickly to her car. She keeps her eyes down, her blond hair covering her face. It's obvious she doesn't want to be seen.

"Alexis!" I call across the square.

She jerks her head up automatically, scanning the area. I wave my arm at her.

Her eyes focus on me for a brief moment, then slide away. I'm sure she saw me, but she hurries the last few steps to her car.

She's alone, no stroller or baby carrier. I wonder if Walker is in the car already or if she left him with a sitter.

I cross the street towards her. I want to wave and call again, but before I even reach the courthouse side of the street, she pulls away. I watch her drive away, baffled by her sudden appearance and her quick departure.

I hurry across the square to the street she was walking down. I scan the doors of the buildings. This side of the square is similar to my side. A few storefronts that are doing business, interspersed with a few empty places. A cafe on the corner has tables outside to eat at, and a few tables are occupied. I scan the faces but don't recognize anyone that Alexis might have been eating with. Of course, if she was here meeting friends for lunch, her friends would be gone already, too.

The only other occupied spaces are a second-hand store, an insurance agency, and a church.

None of them seem likely places for Alexis to be visiting this morning. None of them seem like places she'd be slinking away from, hiding from me.

I glance back to the cafe, wanting to question the hostess. I listen to my tattoo for guidance, but it has stopped tingling and no direction from God echoes in my head.

Alexis is a grown woman and whatever she's up to is her business.

Except if it hurts my brother.

My sudden surge of loyalty surprises me.

Thinking of Dustin reminds me of the autopsy report that is happening in a few minutes.

"How can I get in?" I ask the sun.

The sun shines bright and warm but has no answers.

I cross the square back to my car. I should go into the shop and check on Mom. I should focus on work, return a few calls that have been waiting in my voice mail. I should do any number of things.

Instead, I drive to the coroner's office, hoping

a plan will form once I get there.

I park my Charger next to Dustin's cruiser and sit for a moment in the parking lot. My better sense is attempting to talk me out of going inside. "Just wait for them to come out and ask them what she said," I mutter to myself.

"They won't tell you. This man shot at you, you have a right to know," my stubborn side argues.

"Even if you get in, she won't tell you anything," my smarter self argues back.

I remain in the car, disgusted with myself for coming here. How many times have I ran off and gotten myself into trouble? There's no way to sneak into the coroner's.

"Grow up," I mutter.

I know I should drive away, but I can't seem to put the car in reverse and leave. I stare at the door, wanting to go in.

I'm saved from deciding by the ringing of my phone.

"Hey, Gabby Girl, I figured you would stop by this morning?" Mom says. "Man what a night."

A potted, ornamental tree sits outside the glass door and I watch it sway in the slight breeze as I talk. "I went to the museum to meet with Gene this morning," I hedge.

"Where are you now?" An innocent question that fills me with guilt.

"I'm waiting for Lucas and Dustin." True, if not the whole truth.

"Why do you sound so guilty?"

Can't fool a mother.

"I'm not guilty," I lie. "I'm just waiting in a parking lot."

"Waiting where?"

"The coroner's office," I answer sheepishly.

"I thought the coroner didn't like you. I doubt she'll appreciate you showing up."

I don't like getting caught like a little girl.

"Well, I want to know what they found out about David Benson."

"Why would you need to go to the coroner's?" Mom asks, then gasps. "Oh no. He's dead? He died?"

"Yes. I don't know much more. That's why I want to hear the coroner's report."

Mom's voice is choked with sadness. "If he

was running from us, then we are responsible for his death."

"No. Stop that. If he fell, that is not our fault. The man shot at us, Mom. With a gun. If he was running from us, that's his doing."

She sniffles into the phone.

"Still. It's sad he's dead."

I wonder at my callousness that I'm not as shaken up as she is. The potted plant I've been staring at blurs with tears, but they aren't tears for David. They're tears for my loss of compassion.

"Do you think I'm a monster?"

I didn't know the words were coming until they leave my lips.

"Why would you say that?" Mom gasps.

"When Lucas told me David Benson died, I barely even flinched. Yesterday, I found Jason shot and shoved in a box and all I could think about was that I didn't get a good reading from him." It's my turn to sniffle into the phone.

"After everything you've been through, it's only normal that you'd have a thick skin."

I wipe at my nose with a drive-thru napkin I find in the center console of my car. "So thick that I don't even care?"

"If you didn't care, you wouldn't be doing everything you can to figure out what happened to Jason and now David."

"David probably shot Jason."

"But why?"

I sniffle again and whine, "I have no idea. That's the problem. None of this makes sense."

"Murder rarely does, darling."

The glass door suddenly opens and I see Lucas and Dustin. I quickly wipe at my eyes with the napkin. "Mom, the guys are coming out now. Sorry about crying all over you."

"You never have to apologize to me," Mom says.

Dustin sees me in my car and meets my eyes through the windshield. "Dustin just spotted me. He looks ticked. Wish me luck." I hang up the phone and rub my gloved hands over my face, hoping any signs that I was crying are gone.

Lucas follows Dustin's laser gaze and his back stiffens.

I climb out of the car and meet them.

"What are you doing here?" Dustin growls.

"I wanted to hear about the report." I keep my eyes down, submissive, hoping that will gain me some leverage.

"At least you didn't come inside," Dustin concedes. I send a quick prayer of thanks to Mom for distracting me from that plan.

"So what did you find out?" I get to the point. "Did he die from the fall like we thought?"

"Yes," Lucas says simply. "You know we are not supposed to be telling any of this to anyone."

"And you know that man shot at me and Mom last night and then died at my back door. Doesn't that give me the right to some information?"

"No, it doesn't," Dustin says. "You are not involved in this investigation, Gabby. How many times do I have to tell you that?"

The glass door behind them opens. I flinch when I see Gomez. "What is she doing here?" she barks so loudly it echoes across the parking lot.

"She was just leaving," Dustin says.

"You detectives," Gomez shakes her head in disgust. "Why not just invite her into my lab?" she says sarcastically.

I've had enough of all of them. "I'm just trying to help," I snap.

"We don't need your kind of help," Gomez

says, joining Dustin and Lucas. The three of them stand next to each other, facing me. I feel cornered and left out. Not a good combination for keeping my tongue in check.

"I've helped before," I point out. "There are some things only I can figure out."

"Not this time," Gomez counters. "This is open and shut. Benson has gunshot residue on his hands, so he's the one that shot at you." The look on her face seems to say 'too bad he missed'.

"That doesn't prove he shot Jason Garafolo," I say.

"Doesn't it?" she asks. "What are the odds that two people are in the same place within a day of each other shooting at people? Let alone the stolen property in his pocket." She tosses her braid over her shoulder. "Plus, Benson's prints are on the trunk. I don't need to be psychic to put all that together."

"But why did he shoot Jason?" I ask, hating the whine in my voice.

Gomez takes a step closer, "From what I hear, gambling debts could be at play, or maybe something else. The why is none of your concern. That is for the detectives to figure out. That is a police matter, not a matter for a freak like you."

Gomez's face instantly turns crimson when she realizes what she said out loud.

"Dr. Gomez," Lucas snaps in my defense. "That is uncalled for."

"So the truth comes out," I say, feeling smug at pushing the stoic woman.

Gomez tosses her braid again in defiance, raises her chin. "You have made a laughing stock of us, of the whole police department. Do you think we can't solve a murder without your hocus pocus? We just did."

I look to Lucas and then to Dustin for backup. They wear identical expressions of surprise at Gomez's venom.

"What I do is not hocus pocus," I retort.

"Hocus pocus, mumbo jumbo. Whatever you call it, we don't need it." With a final toss of her braid, Gomez storms away.

I want to call after her, but the sting of her words is finally settling in and I have nothing to say.

I turn my hurt on the men. "Thanks for standing up for me," I say sarcastically. "Glad I can count on you two."

"Gabby," Lucas tries.

The tears that so recently stung my eyes return. "Don't. You had your chance." I turn away from them and retreat to my car. Anger stirs my tongue. "By the way, Brother," I add sarcastically as I pull open my door. "I saw Alexis this morning. She was on the square and tried to hide from me."

His face turns pale and a sick feeling of satisfaction fills my belly.

I slam the door shut and peel out of the parking lot. Luckily I don't see Gomez walking to her car or I'm not sure I wouldn't have tried to run her over.

Chapter 20

GABBY

I drive on autopilot, too upset to pay much attention to the road. Soon, I find myself on the country road leading to Grandma Dot's. I slow as I pass Mr. Sickmiller's place. The old man is nowhere to be seen.

Getting an idea, I turn around in the next driveway and then park at the end of Sickmiller's drive.

The slam of my door is loud in the afternoon quiet. It seems like days since I was last here, although it was just yesterday morning. The weeds at the side of the road are trampled, a path cleared to where we found the trunk. I cross the road and gingerly make my way down the ditch bank.

The indentation in the dirt shows where the trunk first came to a stop. I kneel next to the spot. I don't have high hopes for what I'm about to do, but after the insults from Gomez, I feel the need to redeem myself.

I slip off both gloves for good measure, close my eyes and turn my face to the sun. "God. I know this case seems closed, but I don't think so. Please show me what I need to see, let me hear what I need to hear."

With my mind open and my eyes closed, I press my hands to the dirt where the trunk had laid.

The ground tingles a little, but no vision comes. "Please, show me something," I beg.

The same blond I saw the first time shimmers through my mind, then disappears.

Useless. I'm beyond useless.

I open my eyes and blink at the sun. "Why?" I demand of God. "Why can't you show me what I need?"

Frustrated and angry, I push to my feet, stomp on the weeds. "Fine!" I shout at the sky. "Don't show me. I'll figure it out on my own."

I march up the ditch bank and back to my car.

I hit the steering wheel in anger and drive the last mile to Grandma Dot's.

Jet meets me in the driveway and I find Grandma and Mrs. Mott sitting on the porch swing. A lovely sight.

"Gabriella?" Grandma's voice is full of concern. "I didn't expect to see you today."

I pick Jet up and hide my angry face in his fur. "I didn't know I was coming." Jet wiggles to be put down then jumps on Mrs. Mott's lap.

"I've been sharing my cookies with him," she explains as if she needs to apologize for the dog leaving me.

I sit on a step, my back to the women.

"What's wrong?" Grandma asks.

"I don't want to talk about it," I mope.

I hear the swing creak as Grandma pushes against the porch to make it swing. She turns her attention back to Mrs. Mott, talking about some client, ignoring me, giving me space.

I listen for a few minutes, not paying attention.

"You know what that coroner told me today?" I interrupt their gossip.

"What, dear?" Mrs. Mott takes the bait.

"She said that I was a freak." I choke on the word. "She called what I do hocus pocus and that it made a laughing stock of the police force."

"That woman is just jealous," Mrs. Mott says.

I turn to look at Grandma who hasn't yet replied. Her face is pinched in anger. "Good thing I don't do her hair or I'd cut that braid right off."

"At least you two stand up for me. Lucas and Dustin just stood there and let her say it."

Mrs. Mott makes a sound of disgust. Grandma says, "They have a fine line to walk, you know that. Gomez has a lot of power."

"I thought I had powers, but I have nothing on this case." I rub my face in frustration.

I then tell them about David Benson stealing from the museum, shooting at Mom and me, and then falling to his death. I explain about his prints being on the trunk, how he supposedly killed Jason.

"You don't think that's what happened?" Grandma asks.

"It doesn't make sense to me. And none of it matches the visions I've had. Of course, I think my powers are broken or something. None of my visions have been right."

"You saw Benson in the alley," Grandma points out.

"But I didn't know that's what I saw. The poor man laid there broken and dying and I was upstairs asleep on Mom's couch." My voice is rising to an alarming level. "What am I going to do if I don't have my abilities?"

The question I've been avoiding.

"Gabriella, that's enough of that." Grandma's voice is sharp and undeniable. I push my lips together to keep them from quivering. "You haven't lost your abilities and you know it."

I keep my back to them, gaze over the field, empty and dry as my heart. Jet takes pity on me and leaves Mrs. Mott's lap to climb into mine. I pull him close, taking comfort in his small snuggles.

"What if I do?" I ask miserably.

"We'll deal with that if it ever happens. For now, trust what you've seen. Trust that God needs you to do His work. That's the whole point of this, remember?"

I bow my head to Jet's fur. She's right. For God.

"I don't know what I'm supposed to be seeing.

Just now, I went to where I found the trunk and tried to pick something up. All I saw was the same blond woman I saw when I touched Jason the first time."

"Who is she?" Mrs. Mott asks.

I turn on the step to face the women. "I have no idea." Something clicks in my mind. "The weird thing is, Gene Trimble said he saw a blond woman in the museum, but she disappeared. He's sure she's a ghost."

"If that building is haunted, I would have known it. I did have a beauty shop there for years, remember? I never got a sense of ghosts floating around."

"Gene says he hears kids laughing and footsteps and the general sense of someone in the museum. Of course, then there's all the stuff that's been moved or stolen and replaced."

"Ghosts don't normally steal," Grandma points out.

"David Benson stole a watch. It was in his pocket when he fell."

"So he's the thief. What about the ghost? What else has been going on over there?" Grandma pushes.

I think about all the odd occurrences over the last few days. "Mitzie at the bakery said she's had baked goods go missing at night. She thought her employees were taking them, but she's sure no one has been there. And her truck was seen out here yesterday morning, but she swears she didn't drive it."

"Ghosts don't eat donuts," Mrs. Mott points out. "Of course, with the history of that building, I wouldn't be surprised if it was haunted."

Grandma and I both look at her in surprise. "What do you mean?" I ask. "I haven't sensed any history. Of course, I keep my gloves on tight unless I'm doing a reading for someone."

Mrs. Mott looks from me to Grandma, her purple hair bouncing in her excitement. "I can't believe you don't know. I always thought they should put up a plaque or something. Not much of interest happens around River Bend. Well, at least until lately."

"Are you going to tell us or not?"

"The speakeasy," Mrs. Mott says with satisfaction. "Back during prohibition, there was a speakeasy in the building. During the day, they made auto parts in the place, at night there was a secret bar upstairs."

Grandma stops the swing and turns on the red floral cushion to face her friend. "I never saw anything like that in all the years I've owned the place."

"It's hidden. That's the point. My grandpa told me about it."

"I don't believe it. I would have seen something."

Mrs. Mott shrugs, "Believe it or not. Grandpa wouldn't lie. He even went there a few times. Said there was a secret entrance to the third floor and a narrow passageway that led to the bar."

"On the third floor? I was just up in the attic area of both the shop and of the museum and didn't see anything."

Mrs. Mott widens her eyes in exasperation. "What part of secret passage don't you understand?"

"Okay, so what does this have to do with the case?"

Mrs. Mott shrugs and sits back against the cushions of the swing. "How should I know? I'm just telling you that some shady stuff went down in that place way back when, so if there was a ghost, I wouldn't be surprised."

"You don't believe in ghosts, do you?" Grandma Dot asks.

"I believe in a lot of things I never used to," she nods to my hands. "The universe is vast and amazing," she adds.

I'm thinking over all the ramifications of Mrs. Mott's secret passageway. It would explain how the trunk was taken out of the museum although I followed it to a wall and the wardrobe. If that was the door to the passageway, it would also explain how David Benson got away from Mom and me and how he was able to break into the museum and take things without being seen.

"Do you know where the bar was? Which part of the building?"

"Grandpa wasn't that specific. I imagine it's in one of the empty stores."

"There's a few of those to choose from. Between me and the bakery and between the clothing store and me. Lucas said they didn't search those places when looking for the gun."

"There's a missing gun?" Grandma asks, exasperated. "Gabriella, it could be dangerous there." Grandma clutches at her hem. "Emily is there right now."

"Grandma, they're pretty sure David is the one that shot Jason and the one that shot at us. He isn't going to use a gun now."

"What if they're wrong? You've never been wrong and you don't believe he did it."

I hadn't said that out loud, but leave it to Grandma to read my mind.

"Don't worry about Mom. I just talked to her an hour or two ago."

Grandma jumps from the swing and goes into the kitchen. She returns with her cell phone to her ear.

"It's ringing," she says, worry etched on her face. After a moment, she adds, "She's not answering."

"She's probably just in the bathroom or something." I don't believe my own words. Grandma's concern is contagious.

She hangs up the phone, then dials Mom again. After a moment, she fairly shouts into the phone, "Why didn't you answer? You nearly scared me to death."

I relax on the step, feeling foolish for letting Grandma's worry get the best of me.

232

"A goldfish?" Grandma covers the phone and addresses me. "She's going to a store to buy a goldfish. She wants to know if that's okay with you."

"Of course it is." I have to smile as I pet Jet and think of Chester. This family loves our pets. "Tell her I'll stop by later tonight. I want to check out this secret passage."

Chapter 21

EMILY

Gabby's question, "Do you think I'm a monster," shakes me. I haven't been able to be a mother to her for years. Now that I'm home, her pain tears me more than I would imagine. Her monthly visits to me in the prison have kept us somewhat close, kept me in the general loop of her life, but I haven't been there to help her through life's trials.

I haven't been her mother.

A necessary injury I intend to remedy with all the ability I have.

Hearing the desperate note in her voice today sinks home what she's been through. Makes me yearn to hold her, to smooth her hair, and soothe her soul.

My car has been blocked by the crime scene tape in the back alley, but a quick look out the window and I see the yellow tape has been taken down.

I grab my keys, lock the shop door behind me and head for my car.

In the alley, my curiosity gets the better of me and I look next to the dumpster where David Benson fell to his death.

There's a small amount of blood staining the cracked asphalt.

It is not the first time I've seen blood spilled from violence. You can't spend years in maximum security and not see things best left unremembered. It is the first spilled blood I feel I may be responsible for.

I look up to the roof. The stone walls appear to extend a few feet above the actual roof, a short wall topped with bricks. Some of the bricks have crumbled. I imagine David running from us, tripping, falling against the crumbling brick to his death.

Running from us?

Seeing how far from the museum this spot

actually is, it's hard for me to believe he'd be running from Gabby and me. He did have a gun. He was the one that shot at us, after all.

"What were you running from?" I ask the crumbling brick. I don't have Gabby's ability to sense things. I'm left with only unanswered questions.

And a need to see my daughter.

Once in my car, I realize I have no idea where to find her. I don't know where the coroner's office is. Gabby shouldn't be there, and I don't need to show up there, too. I could call her and ask to go to lunch or something, but I don't want to be too clingy.

I could go to Mom's farm and hang out there.

I moved to this apartment for freedom, for autonomy. Suddenly the freedom feels overwhelming.

I climb out of the car and go back to the apartment. The click of the lock behind me is unsettlingly familiar and soothing. The apartment is small but I still feel exposed. I go into the tiny bedroom and lock that door, too. The lock is on the inside, but the size of the room feels like home. I sit on the bed and stare at the floor, a usual past-time.

The small patch of light shining onto the worn carpet slowly slides across the floor, marking time. I watch the patch of light, thankful for the small link to the outside, not ready for the entire sky.

The loneliness that fills me is also unsettling familiar and soothing. I don't know how to shake it.

Maybe a pet? Something easy.

My new cell phone rings in the living room. A gift from Mom the day I got released. "I want to be able to talk to you at any time," she'd said.

She could have talked to me when she visited, but her visits tapered off after the first few years. "Too painful for her," Gabby had explained.

I let the phone ring and wrap my arms across my chest to soothe myself, disturbed by my dark mood.

The phone stops ringing but begins again a moment later. I look at the patch of sun on the floor, it has moved to the side of the bed, no longer a perfect square of brightness to stare at.

With a sigh, I let myself out of the cell-like room and answer the phone.

I'm greeted by Mom shouting at me for not answering. I want to shout back, "Why didn't you come to visit more?" but bring up an entirely different subject. "Do you think Gabby would mind if I got a goldfish for a pet?"

Mom asks Gabby if it's okay, and I realize with a pang that Gabby went to the farm instead of here. I yearned for her, and she went to her grandma's.

I hear my girl's voice in the background saying it's okay and that she'll come by later tonight.

Tonight. I have hours to fill. I wrap up my conversation with Mom and stand alone in my new living room. Dozens of pictures stare at me from the walls. "Surrounded by love," we'd said as we hung the pictures.

The pictures are of love, but also of moments I missed. I didn't take any of the pictures. I wasn't part of any of the events where they were taken. Even the wedding photo of Dustin and Alexis is new to my eyes. I never got a Mother and Son dance. I wasn't part of the planning. When Walker was born, Gabby showed me pictures of him on her phone, photos I looked at through the grubby plexiglass of the visitor's area at the prison.

For the months I've been home, I have been filled with relief, with happiness at being released.

A new feeling creeps into the edges of my mind, a deep-seated anger at the man who caused all of it.

The man I thought I loved. The man I married and had children with. The man who framed me. He rots in prison now, is getting his justice. But what justice do I get?

The dark thoughts swirl like a flock of birds in my mind and I squeeze my eyes shut to block them out. Revenge is impossible and destructive.

I open my eyes again and look at the pictures of my family. The pictures make my loneliness more acute.

Maybe a pet is a good idea. I grab my keys again and head out for a pet store. A goldfish isn't much, but it's another heartbeat to keep me company in this empty apartment. The apartment I thought wanted.

Chapter 22

GABBY

I sip sweet tea and watch the sun shift across the fields behind Grandma's farm for a while, enjoying the quiet camaraderie of Grandma Dot and Mrs. Mott, listening to their soft chatter. The familiarity of it soothes my hurt pride.

I check the time on my phone. "Crap on a cracker, it's later than I thought. I have a small job to do today."

"Another lost treasure?" Mrs. Mott asks.

"No. Nothing like that. Someone inherited a box from their dead sister. It's an old wooden thing that they can't get open. They want me to see if I can tell if there's anything valuable in it before they break it open. I guess it's a pretty box."

"Sounds interesting," Mrs. Mott says.

"Better be. I'd rather be here investigating the David and Jason case."

"That case is closed," Grandma points out.

I shrug, "I suppose. Anyway, I need to drive all the way over to Maddison to do this job. If I want to get back to look for the secret tunnels with mom tonight, I better get going."

"Maddison. That's a little out of the way, isn't it?" Grandma asks.

"I go where the money is." I stand from the steps. "Mind if I make a sandwich before I leave?"

"Of course not. There's some fresh ham in the bottom drawer." Grandma follows me into the kitchen. "You're serious about looking for this secret passage?" Grandma looks out the window to make sure Mrs. Mott is still on the porch. "There may not be one."

"Something about all of this isn't right. You know I can't stop snooping around until I feel it's all settled." I pull the ham out of the fridge drawer.

"Snooping? That doesn't sound like a word

you'd use."

"Maybe Dustin is rubbing off on me. He's been pretty upset with me lately." I spread mayonnaise on bread.

"He's upset with everyone." I can tell by her tone she's hiding something.

I glance out the window myself. Mrs. Mott is gazing over the fields. "I saw Alexis this morning," I whisper to Grandma. "She was across the square. I know she saw me, but she acted like she didn't. Then she drove away fast."

"Oh yeah," Grandma would lose at poker every time.

"She didn't have Walker with her. I'd guess he was here with you." I point to a sippy cup still half-full of juice in the sink.

"Leave it alone, Gabriella," Grandma warns. "Alexis is entitled to her privacy. It's not easy for her to be married into a family of detectives."

"As long as she isn't doing something to hurt Dustin."

Grandma turns suddenly and faces me. "If she was, I certainly wouldn't be helping her by watching Walker." Anger etches the corners of her mouth.

"Or course not," I back-peddle. "I'm just used to them swimming in marital bliss. It's weird thinking of them having troubles."

"Maybe the trouble isn't with the marriage," she says cryptically.

I add the top piece of bread to my sandwich with a stroke of finality. "You're probably right."

"I usually am," she smiles. "Now go to your clients."

I take a large bite of the sandwich. "Thanks for the food. My fridge is a bit bare at the moment."

"You have mayo on your lip."

"Saving it for later," I tease.

With a pet for Jet's head and wave for Mrs. Mott, I take off towards Maddison.

The trip to Maddison to see the old box is one of the oddest readings I've ever done. The woman with the antique locked box explains her sister was recently murdered and one of the things they found in her house is the box. Something about it calls to her, the intricately carved top intriguing.

When I sit down with her and her young teen daughter, the box sitting between us on the coffee table, I know right away that the drive up here was a mistake.

"I'm sorry," I tell the woman, shaking my head vigorously. "I don't think I can do this."

Her previously expectant face falls. "Why not? I read on our website that you touch things to read them. You haven't even touched it." She nods to the gloves still on my hands.

The energy emanating from the box is like a physical thing reaching for me.

"I can feel the energy from here," I try to explain, playing with my necklace nervously. "I won't be touching it. If you are wondering if there's anything valuable inside, I can tell you there isn't."

"How do you know that?"

"I just do. There's a reason you called me, after all."

The woman is growing angry, but I can't help her. "I thought you were the best. I've seen you on the news several times. You're supposed to be this magical woman."

It's all I can do to not laugh at that.

"I'm not magical, but I do have certain abilities. My abilities are telling me that your box has a bad energy about it." My tattoo tingles and a message blares clear in my mind. I share the message with my client. "If it was me, I'd burn it."

The woman grabs the box and holds it to her chest in anger. "I am not burning it. And I am not paying you."

I take this as my hint to leave. "I understand," I say, pulling my gloves even tighter, then shoving my hands in my jacket pockets. The urge to get away from the box is strong. I head for the door.

The daughter hasn't said a word the entire time I've been in their house, but she joins me at the door. "Thanks for trying," she says quietly, her eyes on my shoes, her fingers twirling a length of her red hair.

I make my escape from the house and the strange box and curse at myself for my stupidity. I've more than once said house calls are a fool's game. I'm now out a few hours of my day and half a tank of gas with nothing to show for it.

I let the strange box leave my mind as I drive away from the house. The entire town of Maddison makes my skin tingle. As I leave the town behind and drive past fields and woods towards River Bend, my heart feels lighter, even as the sky grows darker.

I'd rather deal with a murder investigation than whatever is in that thing.

If there is an investigation left to work on. The case seems closed. I haven't heard from Lucas since the coroner's parking lot debacle earlier today. I hope that he's getting some rest since the case is basically wrapped up, but I'm pretty sure he's buried in paperwork.

I debate calling him and checking on things but decide against it. I'm still hurt that he and Dustin let Gomez call me names. I don't care that they have rules and lines that they can't cross. As a girlfriend and a sister, there should be some lines that don't get crossed in my favor once in a while.

Chapter 23

LUCAS

I watch Gabby peel out of the parking lot at the coroner's office with exhausted eyes. She's right, I did nothing to protect her from Gomez's sharp tongue. I'm not sure what I could have said to stop the attack, but standing there with my mouth hanging open in surprise was not the right way to handle the situation.

I'm angry at myself.

Dustin is angry at his sister.

Or possibly his wife, after what Gabby said about seeing her this morning. We drive back to the police department in tense silence.

On feet slowed by being up for two days, we trudge back to our office. I shrug out of my jacket and hang it on the back of my chair, then fall heavily into the seat. Dustin makes a small grunting sound as he takes his own seat across the desks from me. Our eyes meet for a brief moment and we both break into laughter.

"Which one do you think would win in a wrestling match?" Dustin asks.

"You know my money's on Gabby. She's fearless." I'm laughing so hard tears come to my tired eyes and I wipe them away. I feel over-tired and giddy.

Dustin's eyes water as well and adds, "But Gomez has that braid. She could use it as a weapon."

Officer Patterson walks into our office, "What's so funny?" he asks.

I try to sober up, but my exhausted mind won't listen. "Nothing," I say with a trailing giggle. "It's really not that funny. We're just tired."

Patterson looks from me to Dustin and says, "You Detectives are weird sometimes."

Dustin wipes at his face and regains his composure, "What can we do for you?"

"There's a man here asking to talk to you. A

Brad Grady. He says he knows both victims and wants to ask you some questions."

The humor disappears and we are suddenly serious again. "Show him back."

A few moments later a tall man with glasses enters our office. I offer him the seat next to the desk. "Detectives, thank you for seeing me." He folds his tall frame into the wooden chair, runs his hand nervously along the edge of my desk.

"What can we do for you?"

"I'm here about Jason Garafolo and David Benson. I heard they are both dead. That you think David killed Jason then fell to his death."

I flick my eyes at Dustin. "How do you know all this?"

Brad runs his finger into the crack between our desks. "Small town, Detective. Nothing stays secret here for long. Plus, you guys were crawling all over the square this morning."

I sit back in my chair, unconvinced, but willing to concede that the gossip in River Bend runs faster than the river.

"Patterson told us you had some questions?" Dustin prompts. "Did you think of something after we talked to you yesterday?"

"Not questions exactly, well maybe." Brad focuses on the space between the desks, runs his hand down the length of a long thigh.

I'm tired and have a mountain of paperwork to finish, so I'm not in the mood for vague answers. "Just tell us why you came down here."

"I'm afraid for my life."

The man got right to the point. I sit forward in my chair. "Why's that?"

He darts his eyes at both of us, then focuses on the gap again. "There's no way David would kill Jason. Just no way."

"We heard he owed David money. Gambling debts."

"David didn't care about any of that. Jason was like a pet project to David. He gave him a job and let him keep it even though he wasn't good at it. Yeah, Jason owed him money from poker losses, but nothing worth killing over."

"What does this have to do with you fearing your safety?" Dustin asks.

Brad runs both hands down his thighs this time, his agitation climbing. "We have a bond, the three of us. I think maybe that's why they were killed."

"Jason was certainly killed, but David's death was more of an accident," I point out.

Brad shakes his head. "They were killed. I'm sure of it. Just as sure that I am next."

"You still haven't told us why you're afraid," Dustin says in a tone that hopefully will get the man to be more clear.

Brad reaches into his pocket and pulls out a ring that matches the one David and Jason were wearing. "We all got these rings back in school. They're from the Brotherhood of the Horse. A sort of secret club, if you will."

"At Hartman College."

"Right. We all went to Hartman. And the three of us were in this club together."

"I see why that would make you friends, but not why that would target you for murder," Dustin says.

Brad takes the ring and puts it back into his pocket. "This was a bad idea," he says suddenly. "I'm probably making this up in my head. I mean if you say David shot Jason, then I'm sure you're right."

Brad stands so suddenly, he knocks the chair over and it clangs against the linoleum floor.

"Mr. Grady, I don't think we've helped you or answered anything for you." I pick up the wooden chair and set it to rights. "You came to us for a reason."

Brad backs towards the door. "I'm sorry I wasted your time. I have to go." The tall man turns swiftly and hurries out of the office and down the hall.

Dustin and I look at each other once he's gone. "What was that about?" Dustin asks.

I shrug my weary shoulders, exhaustion creeping back in. A pile of paperwork awaits and my bed is calling my name.

"Let's just get this done so we can go home. I'm still hoping to see Gabby tonight if she'll let me."

Chapter 24

EMILY

Gabby's shop is darkening as I enter carrying my new ten-gallon fish tank and bags from the pet store. The setting sun fills the space with shadows and gives me the willies. I hurry to the steps and up to my apartment. In the distance, probably from somewhere on the square, I hear children laughing. The lovely sound chases the skittering fears from my mind. I lean against the hall wall, balancing the tank on my knee as I open the door to my apartment.

The laughing in the distance ends abruptly, the sudden quiet unnerving.

I let myself into the apartment, surprised to see I left a light on. It was full daylight when I left, and I don't remember flipping the switch.

Maybe I bumped it on my way out. I'm happy about the light now.

I set the heavy tank on a table in the living room and put the bags on the couch. I take out the clear plastic one tied shut with a rubber band and look at the three white and orange goldfish I purchased.

"Welcome home, Cleo, Leo, and Maud," I tell the fish, pleased to have someone to talk to in the empty space. Cleo opens and closes her mouth at me. I imagine she's telling me hello and smile.

A short time later, I have the tank set up, the blue gravel spread evenly at the bottom, the fake plants stuck in the gravel, the bubbling treasure chest lifting its lid every few minutes. I sit on the couch and watch the trio swim about their new home. They seem scared and curious at the same time.

"I know how you feel," I tell them. "Not sure what to do with all that space."

I'm unduly excited about the addition to my apartment and can't wait to show them to Gabby. I grab my phone and text her to see if she was still coming over like she said. I could have sworn she said something about secret passages. With Gabby, I can never be sure.

She texts back a moment later. "On my way back from Maddison. Be there in a bit."

Satisfied, I sit back on the couch and watch my fish. "You guys hungry?" I search for the fish food I know I bought, but can't find it anywhere. I drop to my knees and look under the couch, but it didn't roll under there. It only takes a moment to search the small apartment, but the fish food is nowhere to be found.

Thinking it must have fallen out of the bag in the car, I retrace my steps to the alley and find the canister under the back seat of my car.

A tingle of awareness shivers across my neck and I turn, sure someone is watching me. The alley is empty except for the dumpster overflowing with moving boxes. "Hello?" I call into the darkness.

In the distance, a car door closes, but no one answers me. Skittish, I hurry in the back door of the shop. I stop on the bottom step and let out a small sound of surprise. A black shape fills the doorway, lit from behind by the lights of the courthouse. The dark outline is tall and lifts his long arms to frame his face and peer through the glass. "Anyone in there?" the man calls.

Wishing I had a weapon besides the canister of fish food, I cross to the front door and call through the glass. "Can I help you?"

"Are you Gabby McAllister? I need help?"

I flip on the lights and the man on the other side of the glass blinks at the sudden glare. "Do you have an appointment?"

"No. I just hoped to catch her." The worried expression on his face does me in. That and the hope of a paying customer for Gabby.

"She'll be here any minute," I tell the man as I unlock the door and let him in. The jingle of the bells hanging above the door makes me jump.

"I'm sorry if I startled you. I've already been to the police, but they can't help with this. I'm hoping Ms. McAllister can."

I motion to the red couch, "Take a seat and you can wait for her."

He doesn't take the offered seat but holds out his hand for me to shake. "I'm Brad Grady, nice to meet you."

My manners are rusty, but I shove my hand into his out of habit. His long fingers encompass mine. "Emily McAllister. Gabby is my daughter. You mentioned you went to the police, why did you come here?"

Brad lets go of my hand and puts his hands into his pockets. "I'd rather talk to Gabby if you don't mind. It's kind of hard to explain."

"Not that hard to explain that you're a murderer." The woman's voice comes from the steps. Brad and I spin toward the sound.

When I see the gun in her hand I drop the fish food.

"Sunny, I was afraid you were behind this," Brad says.

The woman shakes her blonde curls from her face, throws her head back, and laughs. "You always were the smart one. I wanted to start with you, but you didn't come."

"I told Jason and David that you wouldn't be happy with the money, that you would want more."

"See, the smart one," the woman named Sunny says. Behind her, the familiar rumble of Gabby's Charger fills the alley. Sunny hears it, too, and waves the gun at Brad and me. "Come on. Let's finish this little conversation upstairs."

With the barrel of the pistol pointed at us, we have no choice but to follow her directions. "Sorry you got mixed up in this," she hisses at me as I pass by, my hands raised. "Don't do anything stupid and maybe I'll let you live."

My blood goes cold. Gabby's car is still running and I hope she'll stay in it, not come here to face this mad woman with a gun.

I walk up the stairs ahead of Brad and Sunny and turn to enter the apartment. "Not that way," Sunny barks. "The other door." The door to the third floor steps is open, the light on. I step into the narrow stairwell, Brad close behind.

Sunny goes into the apartment for a moment, before my mind can even think of running away, she's back with the gun pointed at us. "Get going. Or I'll shoot your daughter before she even knows what's going on. She thinks she's so smart. I have a little game set up for her. Let's see how well she does."

I climb the steps to the attic. There's an open area in one of the walls that wasn't there the last time we came up here. A swinging door that looks like the wall. With the gun at our backs, Brad and I go through the opening and find ourselves in a narrow passageway.

The secret passage Gabby must have been talking about. Waiting in the passageway are two children, a young blond girl, and a slightly older boy.

"Is that the third one?" the boy asks.

"Yes, it is, Ryder. I finally have all three."

"Who's the lady?" the girl asks.

"Collateral damage."

I don't like the sound of that, or the sound of the secret door closing behind us.

Chapter 25

GABBY

I'm about a mile away from the shop when my tattoo begins to tingle. One word pounds in my head.

Hurry. Hurry. Hurry.

I drive as fast as I can to the shop, speed up the alley, and skid to a stop next to Mom's smaller white car. The shop lights are on. The window to her apartment is lit as well, the curtain moves, and the sense of panic that filled the last few minutes subsides. I wave at the window and she waves back.

I allow myself to breathe normally, feeling foolish for my panic. Grandma Dot must be rubbing off on me. I down the last of the gas station Dr. Pepper I picked up on the way home from Maddison and rub at my arm.

My tattoo is still tingling and the hurry, hurry still echoes through my mind. I glance back at the window. Mom isn't there anymore. I slowly put the empty Styrofoam cup back in the cup holder, dread seeping into me.

The shop lights are on, but Mom's upstairs.

Hurry, hurry, hurry.

Hurry where?

I turn off the car and obey the message. I fly through the back door, surprised to find it unlocked. "Mom?" I call into the empty shop. I run up the steps to the apartment, sure she'll be there. She was just at the window, she has to be close by.

The apartment is empty except for a new fish tank. I look at the three fish and ask, "Where's your momma?"

The fish open and close their mouths silently.

I go downstairs to look for her. The front door is unlocked, as well. My fear grows. The hurry is still pulsing in my mind, but I don't know what to do. I step out of the front door onto the sidewalk, wondering if Mom came out this way in the few moments it took me to get out of the car. The sidewalk is empty.

Returning to the shop, I lock the door behind me. Then I see it. A can of fish food has rolled against the leg of the red couch.

I bend to pick it up, but before I touch it, feel the fear.

My hand draws back as if burned. "Mom?" I call, my heart pounding and my voice rising.

Hurrying as my tattoo keeps telling me, I pull off both my gloves and grasp the fish food can.

The vision is fresh and vivid.

The same blond woman, a gun, a man, fear.

I drop the canister, breaking the reading, and scream for her. I listen with all of my senses, even raising my hands palms out. "Where are you?" I beg.

Not knowing what else to do, I return to the apartment, hoping to find a clue. The happy pictures on the wall mock me. Representations of a life Mom missed out on and a life she may not reclaim unless I find her.

For once, I do as Dustin would want and I call for help. Hoping Lucas is awake still after his long, long shift. Hoping harder that he's willing to answer when I call, I stare at the fish as the phone rings in my ear.

"The blond woman from my vision took Mom," I blurt out before he can say a groggy hello.

"Slow, down and say that again. I'm at our office with Dustin, I'm going to put you on speaker."

I tell them what I found, what I saw when I touched the fish food. As I talk, I stare at the bubbling treasure chest in the center of the fish tank. The bubbles cause it to open. There's something inside the trunk, but it closes before I get a good look at it.

"Just get here as quickly as you can. I learned today there are secret passages from back in the speakeasy days in this building. That must be how she's been getting around. That must be where she took mom and the man." As I talk I pull up my sleeve and stick my arm into the cold water of the fish tank.

"What man?"

"I don't know. I saw some tall guy with her in my vision. The shop lights were on and the front door was unlocked. He must have come to see me or something."

"Brad Grady," Dustin says. "He came to see us, too."

The treasure chest opens and this time I'm ready to grab whatever is inside. I scream as I touch the ring, the terror and pain so strong. I drop the ring into the tank.

"Gabby, what was that?"

"I think I know what this is all about. Just get here. Now."

I hang up the phone and shove it in my pocket.

The ring was left here for me to find. Left here to explain.

Using a serving spoon from the kitchen, with a towel wrapped around the handle, I manage to fish the ring out of the tank. I sit it on the coffee table and stare at the red center stone. I know this is going to be bad and I know I need to do it. I just have to get my courage up.

Staring at the ring won't change anything. I think of something Grandma Dot used to say. "If you have a frog to swallow don't stare at it too long. If you have more than one frog to swallow, do the largest one first." Touching this ring will be a large frog.

I slam my bare left hand down on it.

The ring is heavy on my finger, new and unfamiliar. A badge of honor. The other Brothers surround me. The three of them wearing identical rings. A sense of camaraderie I've never felt fills my heart.

This man is now more than a man. He is a Brother. He must only pass the test.

The paddles are raised. The paddles I raised myself against my fellow pledges. I welcome the pain, the symbolism.

The pain grows, crescendos. Don't cry out. To cry out is to fail.

The paddling continues and I fade, grow weaker. Don't cry out. To cry out is to fail.

I must not fail.

An errant blow hits me in the temple and I see stars. Stop, I whisper. I do not cry out. I have no energy.

The blows continue. A sharp pain stabs my lung. My breathing shallows, slows, stops.

I can not cry out. I have no air.

My vision grows darker, my Brothers laugh, unaware, thinking it's part of the game.

He's the toughest of us all.

Another blow glances off my shoulder and hits my head. The light fades. The pain fades. I fade away.

With a force of will, I pull my hand away from the dead man's ring. Sobs rack my body and I collapse against the pillows on the couch. "They didn't know," I whisper. "They didn't know, but they killed him."

I recognize Jason and David as two of the Brothers and the third as the man with Mom a short time ago.

I don't know who the blond woman is, but I know she left the ring here for me to find, was probably who I saw at the window. Things begin to click into place. The "ghost" Gene Trimble saw at the museum, the secret passageways. The blond must have some connection to the young man who was accidentally killed in my vision.

A woman bent on revenge.

A woman who has already killed two of the men responsible.

And now she has my mom.

Chapter 26

GABBY

I'm sorry for the tragic accident that happened to the young man, but I won't let the blond take my mother away from me. They have to be in the building somewhere. The woman has most likely been living in the secret passageways and the speakeasy this whole time, possibly stealing things from the museum.

I sit up suddenly. "Donuts. She took the donuts." The secret passage must extend to the bakery as well. I listen hard to the building's creaking, wondering where to start, where to look. The faint sound of what might be footsteps, might be the usual sounds of a building this age, filter down through the ceiling.

"I'm coming, Mom."

Remembering Dustin's comment about bringing a knife to a gunfight, I grab the largest knife out of the block on the kitchen counter and squeeze it in my bare hand. Luckily it is new and has no residual energies to interfere with the work I must do. I need all my senses to focus on finding Mom.

The attic door is closed, a strip of light shining under. I place my left hand on the handle. A shimmer of the blond woman's excitement climbs up my arm. I'm on the right track.

With my other hand, I pull the door open and peek through the crack. The stairs are empty and I don't get a sense of anyone in the room above. With my back to the rough wall, I go up the rickety steps.

The attic looks the same as it did the last time we were up here. Discarded beauty shop equipment and various things that Grandma Dot stored up here years ago. I scan the four walls for a way out of the room, a way into the secret passage. The room stretches from the windows overlooking the courthouse square at the front to the alley side at the back. Walls have been built on each side to separate it from the other businesses.

I know the size of my shop downstairs well. I've spent countless hours there alone, waiting for clients to show up, worrying about bills. Generally spending time. On especially stressful days, I pace from the front door to the back door. Twenty-nine steps. The counting is soothing.

This room looks smaller.

I shove a beauty shop chair out of the way so I have a clear path, then, starting at the front windows, I pace off the room.

Twenty-four steps.

I turn at the back wall and pace it off again. Twenty-four steps. This room is definitely smaller. I rush to the back wall, realizing for the first time that the front, courthouse side is brick, this side is wood.

A subtle difference, easily missed.

I search the planks that make up the wall for a door or a crack or something to give away the entrance. I listen to my tattoo for guidance but it is still pulsing the hurry, hurry.

The planks are rough-hewn and splintery

under my bare fingers, only the barest hum of age seeps through my skin into my mind. Until I touch a certain plank. A surge of emotion tells me I found the right place. On close inspection, I find a small hole that looks like a knot in the wood but fits a finger. I stick my finger in the hole and pull.

A small door opens onto an ink dark corridor.

I duck my head into the narrow passage and look both ways. Each direction is pitch black.

"Crap on a cracker, which way?" I mutter to myself. With the flashlight on my phone, I try to get some idea of the layout. In both directions, what looks like the whole length of the building, a hallway stretches. I know the hall must lead to the old illicit bar, and that's the most likely place for the woman to have taken Mom and the man.

I hold out my hand and close my eyes. I think of Mom, focus all my attention on her, hoping to get some kind of reading.

"God, please help me," I beg.

My tattoo sings one note.

Right.

Leaving the door open behind me, as much for the small amount of light it offers as to tell Lucas and Dustin where to go when they get here,

I follow my flashlight beam to the right.

My palm sweats as I grip the knife and shuffle along the corridor. I mentally mark how far I've gone, I'm out of my section of the building, past the empty offices next to mine, and closing in on the bakery when I hear a woman's voice.

I switch off the flashlight and am swallowed by darkness. "Just admit that you murdered him and got away with it," the woman is saying. "My brother trusted all of you and you killed him."

Her voice is slightly muffled. They are not in the passage. I take careful steps in the dark, praying the floor beneath me won't creak and give me away.

"Sunny, we didn't know he was dying," the man pleads. "We thought it was part of the game. We had no idea."

"Nice try, Brad. That's what Jason said, too. Do you think it matters? Eric is dead because of you three. If the law won't make you pay, I will."

Once my eyes adjust to the darkness, I notice a faint outline of light ahead. A doorway. I silently make my way to the lighted cracks. I press my eye against the crack and look into the secret room.

I see Mom first, she's on her knees on the far side of the room, her head bowed, her hair hanging, covering her face. I don't like seeing her in such a submissive pose, but at least she appears unhurt.

Brad kneels beside her, his face pleading with the wild woman with the gun. The room has a mattress on the floor and I recognize the pillows on it as the ones missing from the apartment. Various items of clothing and other things are piled against a wall. Sunny has been living here.

I shift my position to see the rest of the room. A bar runs the length of one wall. I gasp when I see two children sitting on the bar.

The children from the vision I got from Jason.

The little girl holds an antique doll. She looks up suddenly at my gasp.

"Momma?"

"Not now, Molly," Sunny says, pacing the room in agitation.

The little boy follows his sister's gaze. I get the feeling they can see through the thin wall. "I think someone is here," the boy says.

Sunny stops her pacing and looks right at me.

I pull away from the crack.

"My son is a cop and my daughter is sort of a detective. Did you think you could get away with this?" Mom says.

I'm thankful I can't see the blow, the sound of the gun hitting Mom in the head is bad enough. "Shut up."

I'm not sure what my plan had been besides finding Mom, but now I run. I'm blind in the dark. I hold the knife ahead of me and trail the tip of my finger along the inside wall. I hear the door open behind me and some light filters in.

A gunshot echoes down the hall and I scream as I run. I wait for the pain of the hit to come, but none does. Sunny missed me.

There's no way I'll make it back to my attic door before she doesn't miss. I press my whole hand against the wall as I run, the useless knife gripped in the other.

The tattoo sizzle infiltrates the pounding fear. God guides me and I obey.

Push here.

I push on the wall and a door opens onto an open attic area. I'm above one of the empty offices between my shop and the bakery. Sunny's footsteps, and her gun, grow closer. I scan the room for any place to escape to. In the far corner, I see a narrow stairway climbing to the roof.

Trusting that the door at the top of the stairs will be unlocked, I sprint for the roof. My sweating hand slips off the knob and I panic. Sunny has entered the room behind me. "I see you figured out the little puzzle I left in the fish tank," she hisses.

I look over my shoulder, the lights from the courthouse pour through the windows, gleam on her curls. "Too bad you had to poke your nose into my business at the museum. A woman has to feed her children somehow."

My slippery hand finally grips the doorknob. I turn it as quickly as possible and the door swings open onto the night. I slam it behind me and run onto the roof. From this height, the town stretches around me, a lovely sight at a different time.

Too late, I realize I'm trapped. All around me, a short wall made of brick surrounds the roof. The building looks smaller up here, the space between me and the door Sunny is coming through too close. I run to the alley side and look down. The police cruiser is parked next to my Charger.

Lucas and Dustin are close.

Sunny approaches, the gun pointed at me.

"You don't want to do this, Sunny. The police are here now. You won't get away with it."

"I never planned on getting away with any of it. I just wanted justice for my brother."

"How do I play into that? Hurting me doesn't help your brother or his case."

"You ruined everything. You found Jason and then you snooped at the museum. David was under my spell until he saw you on the news."

Sunny is walking slowly towards me as she speaks. I glance over my shoulder, the crumbling brick wall growing closer. I hold the knife in front of me.

Lucas, where are you?

All I can think of is to keep her talking.

"But what about your kids? I saw them in that room. Who will take care of them now?"

Sunny grows still. "Don't you talk about my kids," she snaps. "You don't know nothing about it."

"I know they need a mom. I lost my mom

when I was fourteen. It was horrible."

"I thought that was your mom down there."

"I just got her back."

"Let me worry about my kids. You won't be here anyway, so it's no concern of yours."

A shadow moves behind Sunny, a slight shift in the darkness.

"Drop the gun," Lucas commands.

Sunny doesn't turn, doesn't even flinch. She just laughs. "Looks like your boyfriend finally showed up."

The gun never wavers, the barrel pointed straight at me.

Lucas advances on her, his footsteps loud on the loose asphalt of the roof. "I said drop it." He takes another step and the barrel of his gun touches her between the shoulders.

Sunny puts her hands up. With one hand, Lucas grabs her pistol and tosses it across the roof.

Sunny meets my eyes, "You ruined it all," she screams and rushes towards me. Her arms wrap around my waist, toppling me into the low brick wall. I feel the bricks press into the backs of my legs. The jagged edges of the bricks reach my consciousness at the same moment I notice the hot spurt of blood on my hand.

Sunny's blood.

I let go of the knife, but it remains in her belly. She falls, sliding down my body. Her shifting weight steals the last remnant of my balance.

I hear Lucas call my name as I topple over the wall.

My bare fingers cling to the loose bricks, my fingernails digging into the stone.

My legs kick at the air, desperate to find footing but failing.

All I can think is this is where David Benson fell to his death.

"Lucas!" I scream.

Lucas's firm grip encircles my wrist, slippery with Sunny's blood.

He struggles to lift me, his grip slips a fraction.

I look up to meet his eyes. "Don't let go," I beg.

"Do you trust me?"

"With my life."

He swings me away from the building and

opens his hand.

    I fall through the air.

Chapter 27

GABBY

I only have a moment to be shocked that he dropped me before the dumpster full of boxes cushions my fall. I land with a whoosh of air forced from my lungs, then look up at the roof. Lucas leans over the low wall. Even from three floors away I can see the concern in his face.

"Are you okay?" he calls.

"You dropped me!" I shout, more out of shock than anger.

"I know, I'm sorry. I had no choice," he stammers. "You're not hurt are you?"

I do a mental check of my body. "No. I'm not. How's Sunny?"

He disappears from the wall for a moment but calls, "She's unconscious, but breathing." He reappears over the wall. "You sure you're okay?"

I struggle against all the moving boxes Grandma Dot and Mom threw in here, but manage to find my way to the side. I throw a leg over the edge. "I'm fine." I begin laughing and can't stop. "Was kind of fun, really. Wanna drop me again?"

"That's not funny," he says seriously.

I can't stop the giggles. "I know. I think I'm in shock. Where's Mom? I want my mom."

I slide over the side of the dumpster and hurry to the back door of the shop. I run up the steps to the attic, then down the passageway.

I burst into the room at the end and find Dustin with Mom, Brad and the kids.

"Gabby, holy crow, I was so worried. I heard her shoot and thought she got you." I collapse into my mother's arms and the giggling returns.

"Lucas dropped me from the roof into the dumpster."

Mom smoothes my hair and holds me close. "Oh Gabby Girl, I don't know what that means."

"Where's Momma?" the little girl asks.

I look to Dustin. "She got hurt. She's on the roof with Lucas. I'm sure he's already called the ambulance."

"Hurt how?" the boy demands.

I look at my bloody hand and hide it from his view. "Just hurt. I think she'll be okay."

The kids jump from the bar and run for the passageway, but Dustin blocks their exit. "Stay here," he commands. The kids glare at him then sit on the mattress on the floor. The girl holds the antique doll close to her chest.

Brad Grady is pale and hasn't made a sound.

"He killed Uncle Eric," the boy says to Dustin, pointing at Brad. "Momma said so."

Dustin looks to me for answers. I don't have any, but I know enough to nod.

"Is this why you came to see us earlier today?" Dustin asks Brad.

Brad just hangs his head and says, "It was an accident."

"Let's get everyone downstairs and we can sort all of this out," Dustin says. "Good job on leaving the doors open so we could follow you," he says to me. "We never would have found this secret passage without you."

The fall must have rattled my brain. My brother just complimented me.

"Sure you don't want to stay home and go to bed early tonight?" Lucas asks as he puts on his shoes.

"Grandma Dot would be crushed if we didn't come for dinner. She needs to see us all together and safe after what we went through," I say, pulling a brush through my hair in front of his bedroom mirror. "Besides, I need to go home at some point, or Chester is going to think he's an orphan."

The word orphan makes me think of Sunny's kids. They aren't technically orphans. Sunny recovered from the stab wound, but she'll spend the rest of her life in prison for shooting Jason Garafolo and chasing David Benson off the roof causing his death. The kids have no other family. Sunny herself lost both her parents before her brother was killed. The kid's father took off years ago and she doesn't know where to find him.

"I hope the system is kind to them," I say into the mirror.

"To who?"

"Sunny's kids."

"I forgot to tell you. They found an aunt, well

maybe a great aunt, either way, she agreed to take the kids in."

Relief floods my heart. Those poor kids have had a hard enough time being homeless and raised by a revenge-crazed mother. "I hope they find some peace."

Lucas finishes tying his shoe, "Ready?"

"Ready."

Grandma Dot holds me tight and long the moment she sees me. Once she finally lets go, she smacks Lucas on the arm. "You dropped her."

"I knew she'd land on the boxes," he says sheepishly. He's explained this before, but I get the feeling Grandma will never forgive him, regardless that it turned out okay.

Dustin shakes hands with Lucas and Alexis gives me a weak smile from her seat at the table. She holds Walker on her lap. Her face looks pale and she has dark smudges under her eyes as if she hasn't been sleeping. I open my mouth to ask her about why she was on the square the other day, but Grandma intervenes.

"Gabriella, would you pour some tea please?" She raises her eyebrows, daring me to defy her. I go to the fridge and retrieve the glass tea pitcher.

"Gran-Gran!" Walker exclaims as Mom enters the room. I'm please to see she has fully recovered from being kidnapped at gunpoint, at least outwardly. She takes Walker from Alexis and kisses his chubby cheek.

"Hey, Mom. Let me get your picture," I say, pulling my phone from my pocket. The pictures on her wall are great, but I'd love to have some memories with her in them. She presses her cheek against Walker's and they both smile for the camera.

"Now everyone," I say.

We shuffle around, squeezing together, trying to get all of our faces to fit into the frame while I hold the phone out with one hand. I manage to snap the photo, just before the phone rings.

Seeing the caller ID puts a damper on the festive mood of the evening.

Lacey Aniston.

I answer without saying hello, "I already told you, I don't want to be interviewed," I bark into the phone.

Lacey is crying on the other end. "Gabby? I need your help."

Goose bumps climb down my arms. "What's wrong?"

My family goes silent, looking at me with worried expressions.

Lacey sniffles into the phone. "My sister has disappeared and I'm afraid to call the cops. You have to help me find her."

The End

If you loved this book, please take a moment and leave a review.

If you've missed any of the previous Messages of Murder books, read them today. You don't have to read them in order, but you will enjoy the series more if you do.

Want to read another great Dawn Merriman book?

Check out all her books on Amazon

A note from the author:

I hope you enjoyed this next adventure with Gabby and the gang. I won't lie, it was a bit of a challenge to open this series up again. At the end of Message in the Grave, everything is tied up neatly and it looks like a happily ever after for Gabby and the gang. In Message in the Snow, I tried to bring a bit of drama, but for the most part it was just a fun Christmas bonus story, a glimpse into Gabby's life.

Then you guys kept asking for more Gabby. Honestly, I missed her too. She is so much fun to write. She's caring, but also mouthy. She's fearless, but also fragile. Plus, I wanted to get to know her mom better. Now we have. I struggled with Dustin. By the end of Grave and especially at the end of Snow where he saves her, he has become a nice(ish) guy. That isn't any fun. I decided to give him a reason of troubles at home for him to be so snarky to Gabby. Don't worry, I'll eventually get to what's up with Alexis. I can't give it all away right off.

I tried for a bit more of a "crime" mystery for this book, lots of clues to follow and even some forensics. I hope it all worked out. The actual murder plot of this book had me pulling my hair out a few times. For a murder writer, I have a huge problem with motive and struggle with it every time. For me, there's never a reason to murder someone, so it's hard to come up with a plausible motive and make the killer more than just "a bad guy." I don't want you to feel sorry for Sunny, but hopefully you can see her side of the story.

My favorite scenes in this book are the ones with Emily. I am so glad she is out of prison and a full character now. I can't wait to see what she does in the future. How will she settle into the world? Will she ever get back at Nathan for all he did to her? I'm not sure yet, but I look forward to finding out.

My tentative plans for this series is two more books and possibly a bonus (wedding maybe??) book. I will write whatever comes to me the strongest. I have other books I want to write, too, but right now, my head is pretty much in River Bend.

This book was interesting because I didn't have a strong plan for it when I started. I'd sit down and let Gabby take over. It is hard to explain. It is also hard to wrangle her in! I can't wait to see what kind of trouble she gets in during the next book Message in the Blood. Imagine, Lacey, her worst enemy, and Gabby working together. What drama there will be.

I cannot thank you readers enough for the outpouring of support and love you have shown me and my work. Knowing Gabby has touched so many of you that you reached out to me asking for more, or silently kept reading all the way to the end of this book, is humbling. I have always said I have the best fans in the world. It is for you guys that I get up early and type away. It is for you guys that I post things on the fan club and on my Facebook page and my newsletter.

It is for God that I write these stories to share with you.

As always, music is a huge inspiration to me when I write. I wear my big over-the-ear headphones and jam out pretty much all the time that I write. I often sing, dance around my office or twirl a baton to get revved up before a writing session. My newest obsession is messing around with a set of drum sticks I got at a garage sale. I beat on my whiteboard as I think and plan. That's the reason I opened this book with Gabby daydreaming of being a drummer in a rock band and playing along to "Don't Fear the Reaper." That's what I was listening to at the time and I had just laid down my drumsticks.

Songs that are pretty much on repeat when I write:

Bloodstream, by Ed Sheeran. This is Gabby's theme song. Not sure why, but every time I hear it, I'm transported into her. You should give it a listen.

Don't Fear the Reaper, by Blue Oyster Cult

Nicotine, by Panic at the Disco

July, by Noah Cyrus

Anyone, by Demi Lovato

Killer + The Sound, by Phoebe Bridgers, Noah Gunderson, Abby Gunderson

Thriller, by Michael Jackson

Getting Away with It, by James

There are a lot more, but these are the main ones.

I sincerely hope you are happy to have Gabby back. I know this book has been both a labor and a joy, but I love Gabby and any day I get to write about her is a good day.

God bless,

Dawn Merriman